THE INVISIBLE CIRCLE

THE INVISIBLE CIRCLE

Paul Halter

Translated by John Pugmire

The Invisible Circle

This book is a work of fiction. The characters, incidents, and dialogue are drawn from the author's imagination and are not to be construed as real. Any resemblance to actual events or persons, living or dead, is entirely coincidental.

First published in French in 1996 by
Editions du Masque – Hachette Livre as *Le Cercle Invisible*
THE INVISIBLE CIRCLE
Copyright © Paul Halter & Librarie des Champs-Élysées 1996
English translation copyright © by John Pugmire 2014.

All rights reserved. No part of this book may be used or reproduced in any manner whatsoever without written permission except in the case of brief quotations embodied in critical articles and reviews.

For information, contact: pugmire1@yahoo.com

FIRST AMERICAN EDITION
Library of Congress Cataloging-in-Publication Data
Halter, Paul
[*Le Cercle Invisible* English]
The Invisible Circle/ Paul Halter;
Translated from the French by John Pugmire

1

King Arthur is present in the hearts of most of His Majesty's subjects to some degree (and in some more than others, as we shall see in the course of this story.)

Madge Pearson and Bill Page were no exception, and in that late April afternoon in 1936 they were having a quiet discussion in a modest pub near Oxford Circus. Several times, the celebrated monarch crossed their thoughts, while Madge dropped names like Tintagel and Cornwall into the conversation. What on earth were they talking about? They both looked solemn and worried, a rare condition indeed in such a young couple.

It's true that the spectacle before their eyes as they sat in the bay window was grandiose and disturbing. I'm talking, of course, about the extraordinary and fascinating spectacle of the sun going down over London, in a sky full of menacing clouds above a blue-black horizon set ablaze by the fiery disc of the setting sun. In silhouette against the last orange rays was a forest of chimneys and Gothic church spires. It required no great feat of the imagination, therefore, to transport oneself back to the Middle Ages with its crenellated towers and dark, damp dungeons. The scene emanated a profound and mysterious feeling of menace, which appeared to have affected the couple.

At twenty-two years of age, Madge—who appeared on the surface to be a determined young woman—actually harboured doubts about herself to the point of being fearful. Beneath a mass of wavy chestnut hair, her forget-me-not blue eyes and porcelain complexion betrayed an innocent and emotional nature. Bill Page was, according to her calculations—for she had not yet dared to ask him his age, as they'd only known each other for a month—about thirty. She felt he would gain from wearing more casual clothes and glasses with thinner rims, and she detested the way he parted his hair in the middle. Bill gave the impression of trying to look more mature than he was. Truth be told, when she had seen him for the first time, she had hardly fallen head-over-heels, but she had found him likeable enough. And she felt safe with him, which was important to her—particularly since receiving the letter from Uncle Gerry.

'I'm afraid of him, Bill,' she murmured, looking imploringly at him. 'I've always been afraid of him, but I don't think I have much choice but to go.'

Bill, drumming the table with one hand, looked thoughtful.

'You've hardly spoken about him. Why would he make you frightened?'

'In fact,' replied Madge hesitantly, 'I haven't seen him very often, and anyway he's not really my uncle, because my father wasn't my real father and they weren't real brothers either and….' She sighed. 'I think I'd better begin at the beginning.'

'Yes, I think so,' said Bill, smiling indulgently.

'I was only two when I left the orphanage and so my only memory of my childhood was my foster-parents, Mr. and Mrs. Pearson, whom I always considered to be my real parents. They're dead now, as well, as you know. I lost Mama when I was 10 years old. She suffered from a lung disease, which made her very weak. And so my father, to spare her the effort, sent me to stay with my Uncle Gerry for two summers in a row, the two before Mama died. They were strange holidays indeed for a young girl, and I think they marked me for life. Uncle Gerry is only Papa's half-brother. They were both the offspring of Archibald Pearson, who had my father Colin from his first marriage before getting hitched for a second time to Ruth, a very beautiful woman but slightly deranged. She, too, had a son from a prior marriage, called Horatio….'

'This is getting complicated,' said Bill, rubbing his chin.

'Yes, but it's almost over. They had a second child together, who was Uncle Gerry. The two brothers—.'

'Two? I thought there were three altogether, with the first son of the second wife of your grandfather, the one called Horatio….'

'Yes, but he didn't stay very long with them, apparently. He had some kind of mental illness, so they shipped him off to an asylum. So, as I was saying, I was marked for life by those vacations. It was only the second or third time I'd met Uncle Gerry, so I hardly knew him when I was sent to stay.

'Being a bachelor, he lives alone in a sort of castle by the sea in Cornwall, next to a little village not far from Tintagel. Even the setting...' said Madge with a shiver. 'You need to see it to believe it. It's built on a rocky promontory, like a small, windswept peninsula battered by the waves. It overlooks a sea which is never calm and where the raucous cries of the seagulls never stop. Remember, I was a little girl, eight years old, who had never left the family nest before. I was already anxious before I even met Uncle Gerry. In fact, I wasn't frightened at the sight of him—he was friendly towards me—but he looked at me as if I were some kind of weird insect. I didn't sleep a wink the first few nights because of the howling wind and the cries of the seagulls. One night, when I was in bed, I realised "something" was crawling up my leg. I screamed, jumped out of bed, and turned on the light. There was an enormous spider crawling between the sheets. Uncle Gerry came, I showed him the horrible creature and...and....'

'And?'

'And he didn't do anything. He tried to reassure me, but I got the impression it amused him to see me almost out of my mind. I didn't think for a moment that it was he who had put the horrible creature there, but it did leave me with quite an impression. One evening, he left me completely alone in his "castle" on some pretext, and I was terrified. Apart from the violent gusts of wind and the banging shutters, I could hear noises coming from the ceiling. Wherever I went, I heard noises above my head. But there was never anyone there. When he arrived back and I told him what happened, he had the same reaction as with the spider: he seemed to revel in my fear, while assuring me that it was only a nightmare.'

Madge stopped to take a sip of tea, her big blue eyes made wider by the recollection.

'Those were the souvenirs of my first stay, along with a few other incidents of the same kind. It was tolerable, even if barely so. I would probably have forgotten everything if I hadn't gone back the following year. That time I thought I would die of fright. I'll skip the nights filled with strange noises and that trip across the moor with him, during which I suddenly found myself alone at nightfall, lost in that wild landscape. Only after I had cried in desperation for over an hour did he suddenly appear: "I've been searching for you everywhere. I told you not to go too far," he exclaimed as he strode towards me. But all that was nothing compared to the famous night....

'Not far from the village, standing on its own, was an old wooden shed. It had no windows, only a door with an external latch, of the kind which drops when you slam the door. While I was playing there, I accidentally caused the door to close and shut me in. There was no way to get out. It was in the late afternoon, like now, and there was nobody around. I shouted and screamed in vain. Then, at nightfall, when I was in total darkness, I suddenly heard a wolf growling. It seemed to be a monstrous beast and it spent a good part of the night trying to attack me. It would scratch furiously at the door and sniff frantically through every gap in the wooden walls, growling through its fangs, which I imagined to be enormous. It was a nightmare I shall never forget.'

Madge shivered and closed her eyes for a few seconds before continuing:

'In fact, it was a harmless sheepdog which had detected my presence. Eventually, he alerted his master, who rescued me in the early morning. Shortly thereafter I found my uncle who, true to form, claimed to have spent the night searching for me. "What were you thinking? I was sure you must have fallen over a cliff, or drowned, or broken a leg at least. You can't imagine the worry you caused me. I was looking for you all along the coast." After he'd heard my story, he tried to console me, but still with that strange smile... I was quite certain that, once he was sure I was shut in the shed, he'd unleashed the huge dog—whose habits he knew well—and taken great delight in my night of terror.'

There was a silence, broken by Bill, who declared with a frown:

'I'm not quite sure what to believe. Either your uncle is an abominable swine, or....'

'I'm mistaken about him?' said Madge, finishing his sentence with a sceptical pout. 'It's not out of the question, I suppose. It's quite a while ago, and maybe my childish imagination and fear of the dark exaggerated my suspicions. Frankly, I don't know. One thing is certain, though: I almost died of fright at the time.'

'What did your parents say? I assume you spoke to them?'

'Well, yes...but Mama was very sick at the time. I did speak to my father, but he was too preoccupied at the time with my mother's health. And after she died, my stories didn't count for anything. Then I was sent to boarding school because my father didn't want to take me with him to Africa, where he went to open a diamond mine with a business partner. He left and never came back. For months I had no news of him. Then his partner, who had lost track of him, told me not to hold out too much hope, particularly in such a dangerous place. That's already more than ten years ago.'

Bill nodded sagely, then asked:

'This Uncle Gerry of yours, what does he look like?'

Madge looked at him in amusement:

'Poor Bill, if you could only see yourself! You're dying to get your hands around his throat, aren't you? No, he hasn't got any horns and he doesn't spit fire, as you seem to imagine. He's quite ordinary looking, and he must be about forty-five years old. It's true I have frightening memories of him, but they're probably due to my misadventures. The only detail which sticks in my mind, the only one left from my childhood memories, is that strange smile.'

'And you haven't seen him for all this time?'

'Not since my mother's funeral. He wrote to me a couple of times after my father disappeared, but that's all. I know what's behind your question: no, he didn't invite me to stay with him at the time. In any case, you can bet I wouldn't have accepted.'

Bill was still frowning.

'You spoke to me just now about his other half-brother, Horatio, who was sent to an asylum. What was wrong with him, exactly?'

'Some kind of mental instability: I don't know exactly what, but it must have been pretty serious. Nobody ever really told me anything.'

'And, as I understand it, his mother suffered from the same kind of thing?'

'She got depressed from time to time. She sometimes left the house and walked around alone in the forest for days on end. I know what you're thinking: a sort of hereditary mental illness she passed on to her first child and then the child of her second marriage, Uncle Gerry.' She thought for a moment, then continued. 'In fact, he never gave me the impression of someone deranged. In the worst case, he's just plain nasty. I don't think my father would have sent me to stay with him if he'd doubted Uncle Gerry's sanity.'

'Not at the time, perhaps, but there are sicknesses which don't make an appearance for many years. Besides, from what you've told me about him....'

'Shut up, Bill! You'll end up frightening me even more.'

'Have you got the letter with you?'

Madge brought an envelope out of her bag. Without a word, she handed it to her companion. Bill could read, in a careful and regular handwriting:

Tincastle, April 17, 1936

My dear Madge,

It's been an eternity since we've seen each other. Nearly fifteen years, at a guess. I imagine you've changed quite a bit since your last stay, when you had so many unfortunate experiences. Do you remember? I'm sure they're part of your unforgettable childhood memories by now. I hope we'll have the opportunity to talk about all that, among other things, and that you'll accept my invitation to spend a few days here. Please do everything possible to be free next weekend, because there's going to be a very important get-together. There'll be seven or eight of us in all, and your presence is indispensable.

What's it all about? I can't tell you all the details now, but please believe I wouldn't be so insistent if it wasn't so important for you to be here. All I can say is that it's going to be an extraordinary event, the kind of thing you never forget. If you can't come, please let me know immediately, but I am counting on you, my little Madge. You really must be here with us in the castle next Friday, in the late afternoon if possible.

Your affectionate uncle

'So, what do you think?' demanded Madge after Bill had handed back the letter. 'Personally, I don't know what to think. On the one hand, I don't feel at all like seeing him again, but he is the only relative I have. What's your reaction?'

Bill thought for a long moment.

'I don't see anything sinister. But do you have any idea what this reunion is all about?'

'Not the slightest. It can't be a family reunion, because my uncle and I are the only survivors, so to speak.'

'"An extraordinary event",' Bill repeated pensively. 'That could mean a host of things…A marriage, for example.'

'People don't usually make a mystery out of that.'

'Apart from that, I don't see anything bizarre, but….' Bill leant over and took Madge's hand. 'But I don't want you to go there alone.'

The young woman's eyes opened wide in surprise.

'Oh, Bill. Would you accompany me?'

'I'm not about to let you go by yourself. After what you've told me, I haven't got a choice. That's if you agree.'

An expression of relief swept across Madge's pale face.

'Bill, that's wonderful. If you only knew how happy that makes me. It'll be our first adventure together. In any case, without you I'd almost certainly have refused point blank.'

'I'm not going to let you go alone,' repeated Bill, attempting a masculine firmness while adjusting his spectacles.

2

Gail Blake, a Cornishman to the core, yielded to no one in his devotion to his native county. The poet in him loved the calm of the wild landscape: the spectacular rock-strewn plateaux; the vistas of heather ending abruptly at the edges of sheer cliffs; and the innumerable creeks of golden sand. He loved the jagged coastline swept by heavy swell; the sight of the waves breaking interminably on the rocks; the plaintive cries of the seagulls; and the salty spray borne on the harsh winds. In short, he loved Cornwall. As he made his solitary way across the moors and along the coastal trails he could explore the landscape with an interest which never waned; and as a bachelor he could devote his time entirely to his passion.

Besides, it wasn't just a passion. The keen observation and the search for atmosphere were, in some ways, part of his job, because he was a poet. To be sure, his writings barely earned him enough to live on, but his demands were few and his home was a small granite hut in the northern part of the county, near the sea. He was an imposing figure with a long, black beard and a powerful torso, well into his fifties but with the vigour of a younger man. At first sight, he looked more like a pirate or a smuggler than a poet.

The life of a recluse didn't prevent him from knowing a lot of people. Celtic in heart and soul, he attended most of the region's many festivals, often as guest of honour. On the other hand, he nurtured a thinly-veiled hostility towards intruders, which in his mind included anyone not a native of the region. It was not unknown for him, when under the influence, to pick a fight with those whose faces were unfamiliar to him: fights which he seldom lost. When chided for his lack of hospitality, he would smile and his pale blue eyes would gleam with malice.

On that particular day, he was lost in thought as he contemplated a pint in one of his favourite haunts, the *Black Swan* at Camelford. Suddenly, he noticed a familiar figure—familiar to him but not familiar to the hostelry—Professor Josiah Hallahan, who taught history in a college in Bristol, and was well-known for his research into Mediaeval and Celtic England. He was slightly older than Gail, but considerably thinner; despite a long white beard, his cherubic cheeks and almost permanent smile gave him a childlike air.

The two men had met several times at Celtic festivals and quickly became friends. Two rounds of beer were quickly ordered and a lively discussion began.

'So, Josiah,' said Gail in his stentorian voice, 'you're now the acknowledged expert on all things "Arthurian." Those recent theories of yours about the Holy Grail and the Round Table have now been accepted, even though they were a surprise to many at first. I particularly enjoyed your last conference. There was something almost magical about your theories, which left your critics speechless.'

'Do you know what they call me now? "Merlin the Enchanter." It has a nice ring to it, don't you think?'

'Well now,' replied Gail with amusement. 'I must admit I haven't always thought of you in those terms. It's rather flattering, don't you think?'

Josiah Hallahan didn't reply immediately. He seemed lost in thought as he stroked his long beard, but then he suddenly asked:

'Do you know what brings me to these parts? I've booked a room here until Friday.'

Blake gave a silent shrug, so Hallahan continued:

'Do you know Gerry Pearson?'

'Gerry Pearson? Only slightly. Who doesn't know him? He lives in a castle on a headland, not far from here.'

'What do you think of him?'

Gail Blake's face darkened and he thought for a moment before replying:

'I haven't had much to do with him, so far.'

'If anyone had asked me, I'd have said the same thing. Yet he's the reason I'm here. He's invited me to spend the weekend. I must admit I'm intrigued.'

'In honour of any event in particular?'

'Apparently. The trouble is, he's not specific, except to say it's particularly important. That's it.'

'And you accepted anyway.'

Josiah Hallahan smiled wanly:

'Gail, you know my incorrigible curiosity. I've always loved puzzles and Gerry Pearson has always intrigued me. On the rare occasions I've met him, I've had the impression that he fancied himself as King Arthur on his island near Tintagel.'

From his seat in the smoking compartment, Frank Dunbar watched the bleak landscape of Somerset roll by. It is human nature, on long journeys away from home, to take stock of one's situation in life. His own was far from brilliant, to say the least. Forty years old, bachelor, heavy drinker and a career in journalism which had left him totally disillusioned. At what point had the downward slope begun? There was no doubt in his mind: the moment he had met that woman, Ursula Brown. She had literally bewitched him. For a brief second, a misty image of her flitted across the green landscape which stretched out endlessly before him.

Ursula…slender, supple and with a shock of magnificent red hair. The look in her blue-green eyes was unforgettable: mocking, fascinating and dangerously troubling; the deep waters of a magic lake fatal to unwary swimmers like himself.

She and he were both barely twenty when they met on a station platform. She had seemed desperate, her hair dishevelled, as she sat slumped next to a large suitcase. He had immediately diagnosed a broken love affair, and he had been right. They had struck up a conversation and she had opened her heart to him, describing the sudden and brutal way the man of her life had cast her aside. Although she had catered to his every whim, he had become more and more demanding, more intransigent and more cruel, to the point she believed he derived pleasure from watching her suffer.

Frank remembered with crystal clarity all Ursula's bitter outpourings and the peculiar light in her eyes: "Yes, I believe there was something perverse about Gerry, as if he enjoyed watching people suffer."

Later, Frank would ask himself the same question, but about Ursula. In so doing, he had revised his unfavourable opinion of Gerry. For, when it came to perversity, no one could hold a candle to Ursula. During their blissful time together he had experienced the best and the worst, going in turn from Heaven to Hell: madly in love one day and utterly disagreeable the next, distant and openly disdainful when she spent evenings with "old acquaintances." Yes, she had made him suffer, fanning the flames of jealousy whenever the occasion arose. And when the time had come to dump him, she showed him the door with an alacrity which would have put Gerry to shame, for that was the name which came to mind when Frank found himself on the street with a suitcase.

Was the portrait Ursula had painted of him truly the reality, or was the "perverse being" rather Ursula herself? It was not out of the question that Gerry—more clear-thinking and courageous than Frank himself—had taken the initiative to break off first. Which might explain why the proud and imperious Ursula had been in such a state when he had found her that day in the station.

Nearly twenty years had gone by since then. Frank went through every one of them in his mind as the train approached Cornwall, the home of the famous Gerry, whom he had never met. He'd never seen Ursula again, either. Ursula, who had stolen his heart and never returned it. He hated her...and loved her just as much as ever. The train started to slow down. The journalist stood up and went out into the corridor where, pulling a flask out of an inside pocket, he took a swig of whisky. He lit a cigarette as the platform approached. There was a squealing of brakes and the train drew to a halt.

'Taunton, five minutes stop,' announced a metallic voice.

He was getting closer to Cornwall. Despite a sense of excitement, Frank Dunbar remained calm. Suddenly his expression changed, and there was a tightness in his throat. For, among the passengers coming through the platform barrier was a female figure which had lost none of its grace and beauty and which he would have recognised anywhere: Ursula Brown.

Comfortably installed in an armchair in his snug, plush London flat, Charles Jerrold was reading *The Times* with great interest. With his greying temples and his discrete and benevolent expression, no one would have been surprised to learn that he was a psychiatrist at one of London's leading medical establishments. Despite his appearance, however, he was strict and demanding with his patients, who held mixed views about him.

'Incredible,' he murmured, putting the newspaper down.

'What's incredible, Charles?' asked Alice, his blonde wife, a rather large and slow-moving woman, who was methodically packing her husband's suitcase.

'They let that maniac out last month.'

'Which particular maniac?'

'The fellow who killed three or four people during a theatre performance somewhere in the north, a dozen or so years ago. Incredible.'

Mrs. Jerrold straightened up:

'Do you know what I wish, Charles?'

'No, dear?'

'That if I have mental problems one day, you won't be the one to treat them. I think you're much too harsh in your judgments.'

'I know what you're referring to, Alice.'

'All your colleagues say....'

'Let them say what they like. I do my job as I see fit and as I believe it should be done. And, in this case, I think it's running a great risk to let this fellow out, that's all.'

'In this and in a lot of others. If you had your way, half of His Majesty's subjects would be walking around in strait-jackets.'

Charles Jerrold replied with a slight shrug of the shoulders.

'What's really strange, on the other hand,' continued Mrs. Jerrold, 'is that you're not in the slightest suspicious when someone completely unknown to you invites you to spend a weekend in the wilds of Cornwall.'

'My dear, please stop nagging me. You know perfectly well that I'm not going there for pleasure. I'd much prefer to spend a quiet weekend here with you. But you must understand that, in my profession, one can't shirk one's responsibilities when one is sought out for one's competence. And Gerry Pearson isn't someone completely unknown. I'm sure I've heard the name somewhere. Besides, Sir Eustace knows him.'

'Say what you will, I still find the invitation bizarre.'

'Bizarre?' repeated the psychiatrist, raising his voice. 'And why the devil should it be bizarre? The letter is like a thousand others seeking the advice of a specialist. What's bizarre about that? And Cornwall isn't at the end of the earth.'

So saying, he stood up, pulled the letter in question out of his pocket, and reread it:

Tincastle, April 18, 1936

Dear Sir,

A number of my friends having spoken to me about you in glowing terms—including Sir Eustace, whom you know well—I believe I should look no further to find the man indispensable to the success of the forthcoming reunion I am organising on these premises on the last weekend of the month. Those present will include Josiah Hallahan, the celebrated historian, and Gail Blake, a local poet, of whom you must certainly have heard.

The programme will consist of the usual moments of relaxation, but also a singular experience which will require the presence of a man of your calibre. Your superior analytical skills, impartial judgment and profound understanding of human nature are the qualities I am looking for in a trustworthy witness. In order not to influence your findings, however, I prefer not to reveal any more at this stage.

I and my friends sincerely hope you can be with us at the end of the month.

Hoping to make your acquaintance shortly, I remain your humble servant.

Gerry Pearson

P.S. It goes without saying that all expenses will be paid. An early reply would be appreciated.

An hour later, Charles Jerrold was sitting in a first class compartment at Paddington Station. After having placed the suitcase so meticulously prepared by Mrs. Jerrold in the overhead rack, he settled comfortably in a corner seat, from which he could observe the passengers hastening along the platform.

"Always an instructive exercise," he thought to himself, "for those capable of analysing and interpreting the facts; those with a *profound understanding of human nature*. A difficult science maybe, but a fascinating and rewarding one."

3

At around four o'clock in the afternoon of the last Friday in April of 1936, as dark clouds were gathering in the west, the bus from Exeter arrived at Camelford Station and Madge Pearson and Bill Page got out. The latter, burdened with his own large travel bag and Madge's suitcase, walked slowly out to the forecourt, casting suspicious glances in all directions.

'You seem tense, Bill,' observed Madge, in a voice intended to sound cheerful. 'You're even more nervous than I am.'

'I'm wondering whether we'll find a taxi in this godforsaken hole. It would be pure madness to try and walk. The way the weather is looking, we'd be soaked to the skin before we even got there.'

'Don't be so pessimistic. I'm sure it'll turn out fine for the weekend. And in any case, it's much too far to walk.'

'Fine weather? That's not what the forecast said. You're the one who's excessively optimistic. Let's start by finding a taxi. This isn't quite London.'

The wheezing old banger which took them to Tincastle village had indeed nothing to do with the taxis of the capital. But the driver, despite his age, was alert and so garrulous as to put his London counterparts to shame. He was still talking when, half an hour later, he dropped the young couple off in front of the church, an old granite edifice which soared above the modest but solid houses which surrounded it, their thick walls built to resist the fiercest of storms. The church steeple, the gables of the old slate roofs and the vaguely conical chimneys formed, in the greyness of the late afternoon, a strangely foreboding broken shape from which emanated a hostility the traveller could not help but notice.

'I'll leave you here,' announced the driver, shutting the motor off. 'There's a path just behind the church which leads up to the castle. It's too narrow and too steep for my poor old banger. The castle's about a mile up the path, but even a new car wouldn't be able to make it. So, you're going to have to—Hell's bells!'

A gust of wind had blown his cap off and he ran after it. Madge couldn't help laughing, but a quarter of an hour later, as they looked out over the Atlantic from a high promontory, the north wind played her the same trick, whisking away the ravishing little green hat which suited her so well. The effect might have been comical if Bill, in an excess of gentlemanly zeal, had not almost disappeared off the cliff in an attempt to grab it. The incident could have been interpreted as an ill omen, given the unfriendly surroundings.

The place where they found themselves was indeed impressive. The wild and jagged north coast of Cornwall was lashed incessantly by the immense and implacable green mass of the sea. In front of them, flecked in foam, a rocky peninsula emerged from the waves. A medieval manor clung to its northern flank, a sombre and disturbing silhouette under the leaden sky. To get there, they would have to descend to cross a natural arch, surmounted by a small wooden bridge over the raging sea.

'You're crazy, Bill,' said Madge, shivering. 'You almost came to a sticky end.'

'I wasn't thinking.'

'All because of this wind, this damned wind. It's always so sudden. It took my hat as if it were giving me a slap on the head. What on earth persuaded us to come here?'

She asked herself the same question again, a few minutes later, while they were crossing the slippery planks of the wooden bridge. Although the metal guardrails seemed solid enough, the structure of the bridge itself left a lot to be desired: for a distance of thirty feet or so, it no longer rested on solid rock, which had crumbled away at that point. Right below their feet a raging sea pounded dripping black rocks, exposing and covering them by turns and releasing a fog of foam upwards.

'Be careful, Bill,' said Madge, clinging to his arm. 'Everything's so slippery.'

'Actually, I had noticed.'

'When the weather's fine, I'm sure we could cross by jumping from rock to rock.'

'I wouldn't recommend it.'

'On the other hand, when the weather's bad and the tide is high, you can get drenched by the waves.'

Arriving on the island, Bill put the bags down, wiped his glasses and contemplated an immense rocky tower which seemed to disappear into the clouds. Off to his right the path hewn into the rock seemed scarcely protected by a fragile railing. They continued their journey, accompanied by the shrill cries of the seagulls wheeling around in the sky above them.

Halfway through their climb Bill suddenly stopped, put down the bags and, frowning, patted his pockets:

'My wallet! It's gone.'

'Are you sure? You had it when you paid the taxi.'

'Exactly.'

'You must have lost it when you tried to catch my hat.'

Bill nodded, distraught.

'Well, it looks as though I'll have to go back. You go on. I'll catch up with you later with the bags.'

'Only if you promise not to go too close to the edge.'

After Bill had left, Madge continued her climb and arrived shortly afterwards on a rocky plateau with a slight overhang, from which she could view the castle in its entirety. An impressive mass which reminded her only too vividly of the terrible nightmares of her childhood. She stood there for a while gazing at it.

Situated on a rocky outcrop of about two acres on the north side of the island and sitting on some ancient ruins, the imposing granite edifice was almost level with the island's highest point. Built on three levels, it got its title of "castle" from the great square tower flanked by an assortment of buildings in various architectural styles, but predominantly neo-Gothic, which time and the intemperate weather had eroded. It suffered from an obvious lack of maintenance.

It all came back to her now. She remembered there was a hut a bit farther along the path and to her left, and behind it a steep path affording a faster but riskier route up to the castle.

The little wooden construction was still there, a sentinel guarding access to the castle. As she walked past it, Madge heard a gruff voice call out:

'Miss!'

She looked round and saw, framed in the doorway of the little hut, a long-haired fellow wearing a threadbare coat.

'And who are you?' she replied, irked by the man's manner.

'Peter. Peter Cobb. I'm the castle watchman.'

'The castle watchman? My uncle has a watchman?' she asked as she walked towards him.

Peter Cobb looked confused:

'Well, I'm more of a general handyman. I'm only the watchman for today. So you're Miss Madge, Mr. Pearson's niece?'

'Yes, but I still don't understand. Why does he need a watchman?'

'To welcome the guests. That, and to keep the unwanted out, if you get my meaning.'

In fact, Madge didn't really understand, but since her uncle had spoken of an extraordinary event, she kept her thoughts to herself.

'Well, I hope I'm not the last?'

Once again the watchman appeared confused:

'To tell the truth, I don't really know. But most of them are probably here already.'

'How is it that you haven't seen them?'

'I had to take care of some unpleasant business, in fact, so I haven't been here very long. But….' The man was starting to babble. 'But please don't say anything to your uncle, miss, he won't take it kindly.'

Madge didn't answer right away, being too disoriented to think straight. The man's job seemed as odd as his behaviour.

'By the way,' she replied, 'there's one more person to come, who may not be expected.' She described Bill and added:

'Come to think of it, you can be of help. We left our luggage halfway down. Kindly have the goodness to take it up to the castle.'

A quarter of an hour later, Madge was sipping a glass of sherry and appreciating the comforting warmth of a roaring fire. The room was spacious, but not as vast as it had appeared to her in the past. Nevertheless, she was still sensitive to the special atmosphere created by the faded tapestry on the walls (the hunting scenes and the Lady and the unicorn had always fascinated her) and the latticed windows, the imposing stone fireplace, the old oak furniture like that bishop's throne, the studded doors and the numerous pieces of ironwork such as the remarkable chandelier suspended over a great round table which she didn't remember from the past. The one which had been there before was now pushed against one wall, groaning from a sumptuous cold buffet.

Whom did she know amongst the people Uncle Gerry had introduced to her? None, it seemed. None of the four men, nor the alluring Ursula Brown, who bestowed enigmatic smiles on all and sundry, as heady as the perfume with which she had doused herself. And a redhead into the bargain. She wondered what Bill would think when he saw her. *What was he doing, anyway? Why was he so late? Suppose something had happened to him on those dangerous cliffs? Better not think about it.*

She realised Uncle Gerry was smiling at her. He seemed to have detected her impatience and came over.

She found him changed, clearly showing his forty-five years. His hair had receded noticeably over the ten or more years since she had last seen him. But his smile remained the same: bizarrely gentle and amiably inquisitive. The strange look in his eye seemed even more pronounced.

But she couldn't fault his present comportment. He seemed to be genuinely moved to see her again when, in response to the doorbell, he had opened the heavy front door to greet her. His welcome was particularly warm and he seemed to exhibit a fatherly pride when he introduced her to the other guests. No, she had nothing to reproach him about, so far. The only thing missing was the reason for the invitation, and the other guests seemed just as intrigued as her on that score.

'Madge, dear, you look worried,' said Gerry amiably, placing a protective arm around her shoulder. 'But of course, how silly of me, you're still waiting for your friend who's lost his wallet. In any case, you were right to bring him and I look forward to meeting him.'

He was interrupted by the lounge door opening suddenly. Instead of Bill, whom Madge had expected, it was young Peter Cobb who came hesitantly over to her.

'I put your luggage in your room, Miss Madge,' he said in his gruff voice.

'Thank you, Peter. But haven't you seen my friend?'

The young guardian frowned.

'The gentleman you described? No. I only saw those two gentlemen over there,' he added, indicating Gail Blake and Josiah Hallahan, who were deep in conversation. 'They came just after you. Nobody else apart from them.'

'Are you sure?' insisted Uncle Gerry.

'Oh, my goodness,' exclaimed Madge suddenly. 'It's my fault. It's because of those bags I asked you to bring up, Peter. Bill said he would collect them on the way. He must still be looking for them.'

'I understand,' said the young guardian, nodding his head. 'I'll go and tell him.'

He turned on his heels and left the room. Ten minutes later, Bill Page appeared, red-faced, dishevelled and glasses askew. Madge could tell he was upset.

But the cordial and cheerful welcome extended by Uncle Gerry put him rapidly at ease. After the introductions were over, Madge pulled him to one side.

'I was worried stiff, and starting to fear the worst.'

'And I thought I was going mad. First my wallet, then the luggage. Disappeared. Up in smoke. I looked everywhere, until that Peter fellow turned up and explained everything.

Madge hung her head.

'It's my fault. I should have thought before I asked him to do it. Did you actually find your wallet?'

Bill tapped his jacket close to the inside pocket:

'Yes, fortunately. It was where I thought, and—.'

He went quiet as Gail Blake and Josiah Hallahan came over.

'Excuse me, miss, we were wondering if you could help us,' said the latter. 'You're our host's niece. Could you tell us what the programme is for tonight? Your uncle seems to take a delight in keeping us in the dark.'

'What?' exclaimed Bill. 'You don't know what all this is about either? It's incredible.'

'You can say that again,' intervened an indignant Gail Blake, he of the overbearing personality. 'Earlier in the week, I ran into my friend Josiah, who told me about his invitation when I hadn't yet received mine. It wasn't until the day before yesterday that I got it. And, of course, it was very vague. Nothing specific.'

The historian placed his hand on his friend's arm:

'I think we're about to learn more, Gail.'

Hallahan had been following the master of the house out of the corner of his eye. The latter had just sat down on the throne by the chimney. After looking round at the assembled guests, Gerry Pearson cleared his throat. In the ensuing silence, he declared:

'Ladies and gentlemen, may I have your attention for a brief moment. I beg you to be patient, for I'm well aware you're dying to know why I've invited you here this evening. I'll tell you that in a minute, but first, let me introduce you all.'

'It seems to me that's already happened,' exclaimed Josiah Hallahan.

Pearson nodded and blinked his eyes in agreement.

'Your conventional names, yes, I know. But from this moment on, we're in a different universe, the universe of King Arthur and the Knights of the Round Table. For this castle, whatever you may say or think, is that of Uther Pendragon, Arthur's father, and where, one cold and wintry night, he placed his young son in the care of his friend Merlin the Enchanter, in order to protect him from conspiracies that he—not without reason—suspected. I'm not talking about the current construction, but the foundations. We'll come back to that.'

'Yes, we'll come back to that,' repeated Gail Blake, with a touch of irony.

Pearson smiled at the poet and continued:

'Well, let's start with you. With your stature, your black beard and your spirited character, you will be Sir Pellinore, the powerful knight who put King Arthur to the test in a famous fight.'

Blake nodded in amusement.

Pearson turned to Ursula Brown:

'You, my dear, could be none other than Morgan le Fay, who detested her brother Arthur and never ceased to do him harm by inventing all kinds of Machiavellian plots against him.'

Ursula Brown opened her mouth to reply, but Uncle Gerry was already on to the next:

'And you, Frank Dunbar, are Accolon, the stupid knight in love with Morgan le Fay and totally devoted to her, ready to follow her blindly into the worst intrigues.'

The reporter was also too surprised to reply.

'You, my niece,' continued Pearson with a sarcastic air, 'are obviously the pretty Guinevere, Arthur's wife, wooed by your servant knight...Lancelot.' (He indicated Bill Page.)

'As for you, Josiah Hallahan, a learned man with a pleasant smile and a long white beard, you're obviously Merlin the Enchanter. A name which you've been given already, I believe, and which fits you like a glove.

'Ah! I forgot someone. There's also Peter…Peter Cobb, the young man who guards the entrance to the castle and whom you just saw. Now, who could he be? In fact, his role is of little importance. He'll be Kay, the insipid adopted brother of the king.

'That leaves you, Charles Jerrold, eminent London psychiatrist. I've reserved the role of Mordred for you. Mordred the traitor. I'll tell you why later.'

Dumbstruck, the guests seemed amused and disconcerted. Seated on the throne, Gerry Pearson smiled down at them. Next to him, the flames crackled in the hearth, filling the silence and bringing a curious light to his eyes.

'What about you?' asked Gail Blake suddenly. 'You're King Arthur, I presume?'

The master of the house shook his head slowly.

'No, not really…Incidentally, he's not far away. Because he's not dead, as you well know. My role will be the most humble of all. That's the best way of putting it,' he added with a sneer.

'We still don't know why we're here,' said Ursula Brown tersely.

'Yes, what's the extraordinary event you promised?' thundered "Sir Pellinore," alias Gail Blake, who was starting to lose his temper.

Gerry Pearson's eyes narrowed and he said quietly, in a calm, controlled voice:

'I invited you all here tonight so that you could be privileged witnesses…*to a murder*.'

4

There was a deathly silence. Then Gerry Pearson chuckled.

'No, don't worry. None of you has anything to fear personally. You'll understand soon enough. But beforehand, I invite you to partake of the excellent fare prepared by the best chef in the village.'

So saying, he stood up and invited his guests to serve themselves and be seated at the round table. The little group obliged, not without some hesitation. At first, there were only half-hearted smiles but, after downing a few fine bottles, the idea that it was all just a game seemed to take hold. And it was at this point that Gerry Pearson, who had been in sparkling form during the meal, asked once again for silence.

'I told you earlier that the stones on which the present edifice was built served as the foundation, over fifteen hundred years ago, of the real castle where the illustrious King Arthur was born. It really was here, and not the ruins on the Tintagel peninsula, as is often claimed. The error is probably due to the great resemblance between the two sites, because this peninsula looks very much like the other one and they are quite close to each other.'

'You know very well that this location is just a legend,' protested Gail Blake. 'Tintagel Castle was never home to King Uther, and, by the same token, not to Arthur either. So let's not talk about it any more.' The smile never left Gerry Pearson's face.

'I understand your point of view, "Sir Pellinore." You can't stomach the idea of a Pearson inhabiting a royal site. You can't accept it. But please understand that this little parcel of land belongs to me well and truly.' He turned to his niece. '"Guinevere," you never met Ruth, my mother and your great-aunt by marriage, did you? No, she died too soon. Well, I inherited it from her and it will probably pass to you one day.'

Madge refrained from saying that, if that were the case, she would get rid of it as quickly as possible.

'But, apart from the land, she also bequeathed a few family secrets which, I can promise you, formally attest to the illustrious origin of these premises. It's true that the construction itself is the result of a series of bastardised transformations by successive owners strapped for funds, with mostly unhappy results. And I'm just as guilty in that regard as they. But forget about its present state. What counts is its roots, the nobility of its roots.'

'It seems you've known better days,' observed the poet mockingly, stroking his impressive beard.

Pearson paused to look hard at his questioner before continuing:

'You're notorious for not liking strangers, "Sir Pellinore," and you count me amongst them. My mother wasn't native to the region, and that's enough for you to qualify my presence here and, *a fortiori*, any claims I may have. And you've never tried to hide that.'

'Quite right,' agreed the poet, emptying his glass with relish.

Pearson turned next to the psychiatrist:

'You claim, Dr. Jerrold, never to have seen me before today, isn't that right? Well, I don't believe that's exactly true. Some while ago, I was going out with a young lady from the London suburbs, whose father was a rich industrialist. A young lady you were courting assiduously, despite having received numerous pointed rebuffs. Then came the accidental death of her father, which caused her great suffering. Shortly thereafter, you had her placed in a special home, as a result of which she did go mad, before taking her own life.'

Ashen-faced, Dr. Jerrold stammered:

'What are you insinuating? And what, for that matter, was the name of this person?'

Pearson continued imperturbably:

'That was your revenge. Against her? Against me? Against the both of us? I don't know. But what I do know is that you had her put away when she was far from being mad.'

'But this is a veritable indictment,' protested Josiah Hallahan. 'What are you going to accuse me of?'

Pearson gave him an unctuous smile:

'You, dear "Merlin"? Who could wish you ill? Who could harbour any malice towards the good old wizard? Everyone appreciates you, Hallahan, you're the most affable fellow in the whole county. That's partly why I invited you, as a counterbalance. You're the exception that proves the rule.

'But I'm afraid you're completely mistaken about my intentions. Please don't think I nurture any hate in what I say, I'm just stating facts. I repeat, I don't hold a grudge against anyone, particularly my dear niece, pretty Guinevere. One fine day, she found herself practically alone, her father having departed for Africa, leaving her with only a small allowance. But she's a big girl now, who no doubt expects to marry soon. Isn't that so?' The question was addressed to Bill as much as to Madge.

'You told me you were an encyclopaedia salesman, Mr. Page? A noble profession, but I hardly think a lucrative one?' Bill stiffened. 'What I mean is, a small inheritance wouldn't come amiss.'

'And you, Frank Dunbar, you're in love with the beautiful Ursula. What I mean is, you still love her. She's the sort one doesn't forget easily. What has she told you about me? Nothing good, I imagine. If she asked, you'd do anything for her, wouldn't you?'

The journalist took his time emptying his glass, then asked icily:

'What are you getting at?'

A broad smile spread across Gerry Pearson's face.

'But haven't you understood? So many people with good reason to want me gone, all gathered together in one room. The victim, the person who will be murdered tonight...*is me.*'

5

Gerry Pearson looked around with a sphinx-like smile while the wind roared down the chimney, fanning the flames in the hearth and illuminating the expressions frozen on the guests' faces.

Blake, a gleam of expectation in his black eyes, was the first to break the silence.

'So, if I've understood it correctly, you've invited us here to witness your own murder. And you're sitting there, as cool as a cucumber, while you wait for your inexorable fate? I warn you, Pearson, if you go on like this, nobody's going to believe another word you say.'

'I just explained that most of you have good reason to want me gone.'

'And that's why we're sitting here gorging ourselves around the table, enjoying the attention you've lavished on us.'

'What more natural, with such eminent guests? By the way, have you noticed the table is round? Just like another famous table. Which means, Sir Pellinore, Sir Lancelot and Sir Mordred, that you are the celebrated Knights of the Round Table.'

'And, since you are presiding over the proceedings, that makes you King Arthur?'

Gerry Pearson appeared embarrassed:

'Not really, though… You know, during the last years of his reign, Arthur had few friends. Lancelot had stolen Guinevere from him, Mordred wished him nothing but harm. He was very embittered, in fact, after so much treachery. A sad end for such a noble individual, with wars as murderous as they were pointless having killed so many of his faithful subjects. Do you know what were his last words, addressed, as he lay mortally wounded, to the faithful servant who had brought him to the side of the lake where the Lady of the Lake and three other women were to come and fetch him?'

'"Fear not, Bedivere, for I go to Avalon where I will heal me of my grievous wound,"' quoted Josiah Hallahan, at once amused and circumspect.

'Correct. But afterwards, what happened to him?'

'It's said he's buried in Glastonbury.'

'It's also said,' continued Gerry Pearson firmly, 'that he's lying peacefully in a magic cave not far from here. And it's said as well that he never left the isle of Avalon, where he's fit and ready to respond to any and every call from his people and *ready to return if the mood takes him*. I could therefore be King Arthur the victim, the one who fell in combat, you see. But there's *the other one*, the one slumbering on Avalon, *who's awaiting the hour of vengeance*. That one you should be wary of.'

At that very moment, a violent gust of wind rattled the windows, like a bad omen. The master of the house stood up, saying:

'Come, follow me. We're going outside, I want to show you something.'

As if hypnotised by so many strange assertions, the guests obeyed without protest, but not before a short delay to allow anyone who felt the need to go to his room to put on a coat, during which time Gerry Pearson showed Bill Page to his accommodation. It was a very small bedroom at the far end of a U-shaped corridor on the second floor of the castle, onto which every guest's room opened. Gerry apologised for it being at the very opposite end from Madge's, but pointed out that Bill hadn't been expected.

The castle was built around a small interior courtyard, accessible through several doors, only one of which opened to the outside: it was set in the western wall, in the right corner of which rose the square tower. Ten minutes after his announcement, Gerry was leading the guests across the badly-paved courtyard in the half-light. Thick, dark clouds had hastened the arrival of dusk and there was a light drizzle. The hurricane lamps which Pearson and Gail Blake were carrying cast gigantic moving shadows on the high walls surrounding them, and, high above, they could hear the wind howling. There had been a feeling of security within the walls, but that vanished as soon as they stepped beyond the postern. On a short plateau, barely protected by a few blocks of stone, rocky cliffs plunged nearly two hundred feet into the sea, from which arose a deafening roar. The wind and the rain drove them back, as if denying them access to the sea.

Gerry Pearson inched his way forward, then raised his lamp to reveal, near the edge, a huge rock in which a sword was embedded.

The yellow light caused golden reflections to glint off the metal which, in the twilight, lent a fairy-like quality to the scene.

'*King Arthur's sword*,' murmured Hallahan, almost in ecstasy. 'The famous sword which only the young Arthur could pull out of the stone, which resulted in him being crowned king. Really, Pearson, you haven't overlooked a single detail. I'll wager it's impossible to pull out.'

'Give it a try.'

Hallahan stepped forward, followed by Blake, brandishing his lamp.

The sword was buried to three-quarters of its length in a large rock which had been hollow initially and was now filled with mortar. It was more reminiscent of a Cornish freebooter's sword than a medieval knight's, with its hemispherical guard and elaborately worked grip, tapering to the pommel.

'It seems to me, Sir Pellinore, that it is your right to attempt it,' said "Merlin."

The poet smiled, handed the lamp to Hallahan, then flexed his powerful muscles before grasping the grip. He quickly realised his efforts were doomed to failure.

'It's pretty well impossible,' he gasped, rubbing his sore hands. 'The blade is trapped in the mortar for almost its whole length.'

'The rock needs to be broken up to release it,' suggested Hallahan.

'You'd have to move it first,' interjected Bill. 'And that's no easy matter.'

'In fact,' continued Hallahan, looking quizzically at Gerry, 'what role does the sword actually play? Is it the murder weapon? Will it deal the fatal blow?'

For a moment, the only sounds which could be heard were the waves crashing onto the rocks below and the howling wind. Ursula Brown emerged suddenly from the darkness and planted herself squarely in front of Pearson.

'Enough of the jokes, Gerry. Tell us what's in store for us.'

'What jokes? I told you what's in store: *I'm going to be murdered tonight.*'

'Very well, if you're going to continue playing games, I'd like to know why I was left off your list of accusations.'

His hair ruffled by the wind, Pearson had lost some of his presence.

Yet he remained master of the situation.

'It's true, Ursula, I did pull my punches a little. I forgot how wicked a woman "Morgan le Fay" really was: perverse, and deadly to any man who approached her. She drove them to despair and despatched them as surely as the angry sea swallows its prey. How long did you stay here in this very place? Two, three, four months? I don't remember any more. You were barely twenty and I was not much older. You were almost the end of me. Luckily I realised it in time and, by some miracle, found the strength to throw you out. I know what that meant to you. The fact that a man had dared to reject "Morgan le Fay" must have been a severe blow to your pride and opened a wound that has never healed to this day. So, you see, you've just as much reason to hate me as the others.'

'So we're all potential murderers?' asked Blake.

'As a matter of fact, yes,' replied Gerry Pearson calmly. 'I repeat: *one of you is going to murder me tonight*. It has to be one of you: there's no one else on the island. Peter Cobb is on guard. His orders were only to let in people with invitations for tonight, which means you.'

Blake let out a Homeric laugh.

'It's too much, Pearson. How do you expect us to swallow all that? Has anyone ever seen anything like it? Not only do you appear to be revelling in your imminent demise, but you're acting like a veritable soothsayer by predicting that it's one of us who will strike the fatal blow. It's stunning. And utterly grotesque.'

'I know even more than that, Blake,' replied the master of the house slowly, as if savouring every word. 'I know, for example, *who among you will strike me down*. I can also tell you that nothing can stop him or her. He or she will strike whatever happens and whatever I do. And this person will have constructed a perfect alibi, proving that he or she could not physically have committed the murder, my murder.'

'And who is this person?' asked Ursula Brown, impervious to the rain trickling down her sibylline features.

'Why, the person who hates me most, of course. *That's to say you, my dear Ursula!*'

6

For a few seconds, Ursula Brown stood as still as a statue. Her blue-green eyes betrayed a whole gamut of emotions and at one point she appeared ready to pounce on her ex-fiancé, claws extended. Instead, she threw her head back, her flamboyant red tresses spread out on her crimson cape, and let out a full-throated laugh.

'You're suggesting that I'm...that I'm going to kill you tonight?' she sputtered.

'That's precisely what's going to happen,' replied the master of the house calmly.

'And that I'll have fabricated a cast-iron alibi? You know I'm not smart enough to do that. After all, you've always treated me as an idiot, haven't you?'

'I never said that.'

Ursula raised her arms in a theatrical gesture.

'Well, of course, you never actually said as much. But you made me feel that way.'

'You're mistaken. On the contrary, I always felt that you were diabolically intelligent. And what I said just now *will happen*.'

'Frankly, Gerry, you've gone too far. You're starting to bore people.'

'You hate me Ursula, don't you.'

'I've never denied it.'

'So let's hope you won't hesitate when it comes time.'

Ursula shook her head. Dunbar was standing next to her and she took his arm:

'Say something, Frank. I don't know how to go on.'

The reporter appeared very embarrassed by the young woman who had just thrown herself, literally, in his arms. But, in the face of Pearson's impenetrable stare, he pulled himself together:

'There's a very simple solution.'

'A solution to what?'

'To prevent you...so that she doesn't....'

'To save my life?' Pearson cut in, sarcastically. 'That's what you're trying to say, isn't it?'

'Yes. All that's needed is for everyone to leave immediately.'

'I say, Mr. Dunbar, what a terrific idea. But it doesn't take into account our friend Merlin.'

Still looking amused, Josiah Hallahan frowned questioningly:

'Are you referring to me?'

'Of course. There's only one Merlin here.'

'Why would I prevent this charming fellow from leaving the island?'

'Not you personally. The fairy you fell in love with, my dear Merlin, the fairy Vivian. Don't you remember, she traced an invisible circle around you, in order to hold you prisoner?'

'An invisible circle to keep us prisoners,' announced Gail Blake in a vibrant voice. 'That's very beautiful, Pearson. At last a little poetry in your prose. Even though it's a well-known legend. Tell us, is the circle in operation at the present time?'

Pearson looked down.

'No, I don't think so. At least, not yet. *But soon!*'

'Are we to understand that it's your guard who's going to stop us?'

Gerry Pearson looked shocked:

'Peter? Peter who'd stop you leaving? Good God, no. He's not there for that purpose, in any case. What's more, he's not a circle and he's certainly not invisible. I said an invisible circle, *a real invisible circle*, just like the fairy Vivian's.'

Pearson's statements seemed too senseless to be worthy of a reply from his baffled and disconcerted listeners. The rain was falling harder now, but nobody seemed to notice.

Madge, just like Ursula, clung to the arm of her companion. The longer things went on, the more she remembered the fears of the past. Although logic rejected all Uncle Gerry's nonsense, her instinct told her that everything he'd predicted so far had come to pass. That same instinct told her to grab Bill's hand and run away from the island. But she couldn't lose face in such a manner.

'Suppose we all go inside?' Blake thundered suddenly. 'Everyone's soaked to the skin.'

'Yes, right away,' agreed Pearson. 'There's just one last thing to do.' He pulled a knife from his pocket and opened the blade. 'I'd like one of you to mark the grip of the sword using this knife, so it can be formally identified.'

Blake accepted willingly, but not before observing that it was a rather childish thing to do. He was followed by his friend Hallahan and Bill, who whispered in Madge's ear that he'd recognise his mark anywhere. Then Pearson asked all the male guests to confirm that no human force was capable of removing the sword from the stone. Blake, Bill, Dunbar and Hallahan followed one another without result. Ursula wanted to try, arguing that the young king possessed nowhere near the strength of the other knights when he performed his feat. But, in passing behind the stone, she almost fell over the cliff, much as Madge's hat had done that afternoon. Once again, it was Bill's reflexes which saved the situation. He dived towards her and seized her arm as she staggered on the cliff edge, pulling her roughly towards him. Pale and trembling, Ursula clung to him like a terrified fledgling.

The others stood paralysed until Blake, having ascertained that she was no longer in danger, announced:

'Well, Miss Brown, you gave us a real scare. A little bit further and you wouldn't have been able to do what our host expects of you, that is to say kill him. That would have been quite a blow for you, Pearson. For your story, I mean.'

A few minutes later, the little group was warming itself in front of the flames crackling in the hearth. Ursula, despite having recovered her poise, seemed more desirous than the others to seek the comfort of the fire. She rubbed her hands together while she thanked her saviour to whom, she said pathetically, she "now owed the rest of her life."

Madge, who appeared irritated, asked her curtly how she had come to slip like that.

'I stepped on a large stake or a thick branch.'

'You didn't see it?'

Ursula shrugged her shoulders by way of reply.

The clock had just struck half past seven when another incident occurred, although less dramatic than the earlier one. While poking the fire, Gerry let out a curse. Apparently, a live ember had burnt his wrist. He took off his jacket, rolled up his sleeve, and rubbed the joint, wincing with pain. He asked his niece to follow him, so she could apply some ointment. They left together and, shortly thereafter Madge returned alone. She said her uncle wouldn't be long, that he had gone to collect "something important" as he put it, but about which she knew nothing. The guests hardly had time to speculate about the nature of the mysterious article, for the master of the house returned in less than ten minutes, carrying an object wrapped in a piece of green cloth.

'After the attentions of my niece I can't feel a thing,' he declared light-heartedly. 'Mr. Page, should you ever be lucky enough to become Madge's spouse, you'll always have a nurse in the house. Ah, I see you're all curious. What's the mysterious object? It's the mysterious object *par excellence*, if I may be so bold. Everyone has no doubt heard of the Holy Grail, the sacred cup which so many valiant knights tried to find. A quest that proved to be as long and difficult as it was fruitless.'

Pearson paused for dramatic effect, staring into the fire, which gave a bronze tint to his face, where an enigmatic smile had appeared.

'Do you remember,' he continued, 'that the cup appeared before the eyes of the noble Knights of the Round Table, preceded by a terrible roll of thunder which shook the castle of Tintagel. The room, which had been plunged into darkness, was suddenly illuminated by blinding rays of light emanating from a golden cup veiled in white brocade. It floated above the table giving out a delicious scent. The table had suddenly become loaded with drinks and delicacies in abundance. Then, after all had eaten and drunk their fill, the cup, as if guided by an invisible hand, faded before disappearing completely, taking with it those marvellous rays of light.'

Upon those words, while the crackling of the fire in the hearth was the only sound, Pearson lifted a corner of the material covering the object he was carrying, revealing part of a round metallic surface which sparkled like gold, and did indeed have the appearance of the famous cup.

'The Holy Grail,' murmured Hallahan, staring fixedly in front of him, fascinated by the golden glow which Pearson had quickly covered up. 'Just how far are you prepared to go with your production?'

'I imagine the magic cup will play a leading role in your story,' interjected Blake in a mocking voice.

'A leading role indeed,' replied the master of the house. 'For it will be thanks to the Grail that I shall be able to return to Avalon after my death. But the hour is near. Come, follow me.'

It was pitch black and on the stroke of nine o'clock when the little group crossed the courtyard for the second time. Pearson marched ahead, still carrying the "Grail." He walked towards the square tower at the northeast corner of the walls, explaining that access had once been possible from the interior, but, at the present time, the passage had been blocked. His hurricane lamp illuminated an old studded door which emitted a mournful creaking sound when he pushed it open. They followed him into a vast space, empty save for a few barrels stacked in a corner. A cold damp oozed from large blocks of granite in which narrow slits had been cut to serve as windows, through which could be heard the murmur of the sea far below. The different levels of the tower were reached by a narrow spiral staircase which Pearson now began to climb, warning his guests to exercise great care, for there was no light and—in view of the narrowness of the steps—they would be obliged to follow each other in Indian file.

The climb inside that dark, draughty stairwell was a severe test for Madge and the others. She clung desperately to Bill's hand, climbing the stairs mostly by guesswork, as she could see practically nothing. From her position at the end of the line, the light from Uncle Gerry's lamp was but a trembling and fugitive glimmer. She found a grim satisfaction in hearing Ursula Brown moan as she slipped on a step.

At last, having climbed several levels which had only revealed wide empty surfaces of the same dimension as the tower, they reached the last stage, the fifth according to Gerry Pearson, but the summit of the Tower of Babel according to Madge. They stood, squeezed together, on a small landing, in front of a door, as solid as the one below, which led to a room with a fairly low ceiling. There was a chimney with a few logs and some kindling wood. On a shelf stood a clay vessel, an oil lamp and some matches. The walls had been coated with plaster, cracked in some places, but with only a few damp spots. Apparently, the fire was lit fairly frequently. The place was sparsely furnished: an old high-backed bench near the hearth, and a venerable square iron-bound chest below the only window, a single hinged frame with leaded lattice-work. There was also a solid iron grill formed of lozenges embedded in the outside wall, a security measure which seemed particularly superfluous in view of the impregnable nature of the spot, which overlooked the ocean from a great height.

Once everyone was gathered in the room, Pearson, after lighting the oil lamp, invited them to examine the premises carefully to make sure there were no hidden objects or secret places. A thorough inspection of the chimney, the window, the ceiling, the walls and the chest revealed nothing that wasn't already visible to the naked eye, after which Pearson placed the "Grail" on the chest and proceeded to light a fire. With his back turned, he said, in a voice interrupted by occasional coughs:

'One might as well spend one's last moments next to a cosy fire. And now, my friends, I shall ask you to leave me. I intend to remain alone, in peace and quiet, for an hour or so. As soon as you've left, I shall shoot this powerful bolt which locks the door.'

He pulled an envelope out of his pocket and turned round rapidly to give it to Blake, adding, after clearing his throat once more:

'You'll find a bar of sealing wax inside and two cords. They will help you place seals on the other side of the door. You can use whatever you want to create the imprint of the seal itself: any personal object like a signet ring or a pendant. Please do it carefully, it's very important. And under no circumstances may I be disturbed during the next hour.'

7

"Why don't they react?" Madge asked herself, watching Bill pace up and down in front of the chimney. They seemed lifeless, in a sort of torpor, completely under the influence of the insidious personality of Uncle Gerry: bowing, as if hypnotised, to his every whim. But what about her?

Nothing. Absolutely nothing. She was waiting for the next shoe to drop, just like the others.

The next shoe? She daren't even think about it. The climb up that staircase in the darkness had shaken her badly. Then the heavy thud of that door closing and the sound of the bolt Uncle Gerry had shot to lock himself in. In the pale light of the lamp, she had watched in trepidation while "Sir Pellinore" and "Merlin the Enchanter" affixed the seals to the door, then "Mordred the Traitor" pressed his signet ring on the one and "Morgan le Fay" her locket on the other. At that moment, under the baleful glare of the lamp, she felt she was witnessing a truly Arthurian moment. She feared what would happen next in this extraordinary evening. And what would be the final outcome.

Murder? Was Uncle Gerry willingly going to meet his death? It was senseless. Everything he'd said was senseless, come to think of it. The invisible circle, Ursula Brown as the murderess—even though that last idea didn't seem quite so far-fetched. She detested the woman, whom she suspected of having contrived to slip on the edge of the cliff, solely for the purpose of falling into the arms of the nearest person, who just happened to be Bill. The woman was capable of anything…Where was she now, for that matter? Apart from Bill, there were only Blake and Hallahan, and they were just leaving the lounge. She looked at the old clock: twenty to ten. Not much more than ten minutes since they'd left that dreadful tower. It had seemed like an eternity.

'For Heaven's sake!' Bill burst out suddenly. 'We can't just stand here doing nothing. It's utter madness. Something tells me something very bad's going to happen.'

'That's what I've been thinking for a long time.'

'It's crazy! Surely he's not just going to stand there and let himself be murdered. It's unthinkable. Despite all the rubbish he's been spouting, he can't be that crazy.'

Madge let out a deep sigh.

'Now do you understand what I've been talking about? With him, you never know what's going to happen next.'

'In any case, he doesn't scare me,' insisted Bill, his feet firmly planted in front of the chimney. 'Although….'

'Yes?'

'Well, it's just that there's something creepy about him.'

'You see? That's exactly what I told you. And—Bill!'

The young man turned round to see his fiancée thunderstruck, her mouth wide open.

'My bag. My little handbag,' she stammered. 'Where's it gone?'

'Your bag? It disappeared just now?'

'No.'

'How long ago, then?'

'I—I don't know. I'm sure I had it when we arrived, but after that…With everything that's happened.'

Bill took a step towards her.

'Now, let's stay calm. I'm sure it can't be very far. Was there anything important in it?'

'No, nothing. Apart from the letter.'

Bill frowned.

'What letter?'

'I don't know. I found it in the letter-box just before we left, thinking I'd read it in the train. But then, since we were completely obsessed by "dear" Uncle Gerry, I forgot about it. It's annoying, for I feel sure it's something important, but I don't quite know why.'

'Maybe your bag is in your room. Nevertheless, it is odd, all these objects going missing, even if they're found later.'

'I'll go and look in my room.'

'And I'm going to take a look at the tower.'

Madge's eyes opened wide with consternation.

'Bill, you're not going out there? Uncle Gerry gave orders not to disturb him.'

'Don't worry, I'm not going to see him personally. But I do feel like taking a trip out there, even if it's only to check the area.'

After leaving the tower, Ursula Brown headed straight back to her room. Almost immediately, there was a knock on the door. It was Frank Dunbar, the journalist, which was hardly a surprise.

'I'm glad you're here, Frank. Gerry's got all our nerves on edge. From that point of view, he's hardly improved with time. Quite the contrary.'

With his rolling gait, Dunbar went over to the chair under the window and sat down. He took his time lighting a cigarette before he replied:

'What I find amazing is that you ever hooked up with the fellow in the first place, let alone living here with him for several months.'

Ursula fiddled nervously with her locket.

'Me, too. But he has changed quite a bit. It was twenty years ago, remember?'

'It's strange: to listen to him, anyone would think you were the tigress who was toying with him.'

Ursula shrugged her shoulders:

'He'll say anything, as you must have noticed. In fact, he's the one who's been toying with us and playing on our nerves. God only knows how the night will end. The idea that I'll be the one to kill him, after having hatched a diabolical plan, is utterly ridiculous. But I'd certainly be happy to wring his neck.'

Dunbar smiled bleakly:

'The situation's rather amusing, in a way. Because, if anything should happen to him after what he said, you'd be in a pretty awkward position. Paradoxically, the more you appear innocent—such as producing a cast-iron alibi—the more you'll be acting the way he predicted, and the more you'll be suspect.'

'That's what you find amusing?'

'No. Seriously, it's nothing to laugh about. In fact, I haven't felt like laughing for a long time, Ursula.'

To hide her discomfort, Ursula turned to the gilded mirror on the wall, and patted her coiffure.

'So, why did you come here? Why did you accept Gerry's invitation at all?'

'Rest assured that it wasn't for the pleasure of making his acquaintance, even though his invitation was quite cordial. What decided me is that you had apparently been invited as well. How about you?'

Ursula turned and walked slowly over to her ex-fiancé. She looked up at him with her blue-green eyes and murmured:

'Can't you guess?'

As they left the lounge, Blake and Hallahan noticed Dr. Jerrold in the open doorway at the end of the corridor, smoking a cigarette and staring into the darkness of the courtyard.

The two men drew level with him and, for a brief moment, the only sound was the rain beating down on the cobblestones.

'Lousy weather,' observed the psychiatrist.

Without further ado, Blake asked him what he thought of Pearson. Jerrold replied that, for the time being, he was reserving judgment. Why had he accepted the invitation? He preferred not to comment for now. Was he a personal friend? No, he had never met him before.

'In other words,' said Blake, looking at the man out of the corner of his eye, 'the story he told about you was a pure invention.'

'Of course. It's not completely out of the question that it happened without my knowing. By that, I mean that I could have made arrangements to put away someone who happened to be his fiancée, after which he invented a scenario in which I acted vindictively. You know, given the time I've been in practice, I've dealt with quite a few people. And this "case" goes back a number of years already.'

'You've put away as many as that?' asked Hallahan, jokingly.

Dr. Jerrold wasn't smiling.

'One rarely talks about that sort of thing, for obvious reasons. But it happens more frequently than one might suppose.'

'I imagine it's not easy to determine the seriousness of a case?'

'Not easy at all,' sighed the psychiatrist.

'Everyone's a little crazy in their own way, aren't they?'

'You're absolutely right. There's madness dormant in every one of us.'

His words were uttered in a strange silence and quickly absorbed by the gusty wind.

'What do you think of Pearson?' Blake insisted.

'You've already asked me that,' the psychiatrist relied frostily.

'Yes, but you didn't answer.'

Jerrold fell thoughtful for a few moments, looking up at the silhouette of the tower, indistinct in the darkness.

'I think the man is conducting an experiment.'

'What kind of experiment?'

'An experiment concerning human nature. But I don't want to say any more for the moment.'

'All right,' said Hallahan softly. 'But I would like to ask you one final question. In your opinion, is our host completely sane?'

The psychiatrist puffed calmly on his cigarette and said nothing.

'In any case,' confided Blake in his friend, once they had returned to the lounge, 'he didn't seem very sure of himself, either. Did you notice he never took his eyes off the tower?'

Hallahan nodded his head.

'Hell's bells! We can't just stand here with our arms folded. I'm going out to watch the tower, but from the ocean side.'

'Well, be careful. You can hardly see anything. And "Morgan le Fay" almost went over the edge.'

At around half past ten, a cry of distress pierced the silence. Within minutes, everyone was jostling everyone else in the darkness of the little courtyard. Blake hastened to fetch a hurricane lamp, whose light revealed only haggard and anxious faces.

Amidst total confusion, everyone talked at once:

'It was horrible, I never heard anything like it.'

'He was the one that screamed, I'm sure of it.'

'Bill, did you hear it? It was horrible.'

'Calm down, Madge, for God's sake.'

'It was a cry of agony. Something happened to him.'

'Quickly, there's not a moment to lose. We have to climb up there.'

Everyone was in agreement on this last point, and it was considerably to the credit of certain of the guests that they were prepared once again to climb up the murderous stairs in almost total darkness.

Once they had all reached the highest level, Blake, who had taken charge of the operation, hammered on the door and called out to the master of the house. There was no answer. He tried turning the knob to no avail and called out again with renewed vigour, in vain. All the guests were now huddled together on the narrow landing.

'Something's happened, damn it,' growled Blake, whose mounting anxiety was captured by the light of the lamp. (He tried to find a keyhole, but the door at that side only had a handle.) 'I don't think we have any choice: we have to break down the door.'

'The seals,' shouted Hallahan at his side. 'Don't forget to verify the seals.'

The lamp shone on the two thin cords connecting the frame to the door, each end sealed by wax. Nothing seemed to have been disturbed, and a close examination—notably by those who had pressed a personal object against the hot wax—proved that the seals were intact. Blake tried to break the door down but he was unable to gather any momentum in the small space, and it was only after a number of attempts that the door yielded with a sinister cracking sound.

The sight which greeted them froze them where they stood, even the imposing Blake, whose open mouth emitted no sound.

To their right, the open window banged noisily in the wind. The flames crackling peacefully in the hearth illuminated the strange immobility of the corpse which lay on the floor, not far from the chest. Its head, covered by a cloth still licked by flames, gave out smoke and a nauseous smell. A sword was planted between its shoulders, the twin of the one stuck in the rock: the famous sword of King Arthur.

8

Dr. Jerrold stood up from a kneeling position and shook his head.

'He's dead, there's no doubt about it. And not for very long, either: the body is still warm. And with that sword, according to the evidence. As for that cloth....'

He indicated the dark piece of fabric, partly consumed, which had covered the corpse's head and which Blake had hurriedly removed and thrown in a corner of the room.

The body was lying curled up on its stomach, the feet not far from the iron-bound chest and the head, left cheek to the floor, close to the chimney. One arm was under the body and the other was flung out to the right. Even more horrible than the sight of the sword planted in its back was the head, seriously burnt by the blazing cloth. What with the charred hair and the cuts and blisters of the face, it was barely recognisable.

'Murdered?' asked Madge hesitatingly, standing behind Bill.

Dr. Jerrold stared at her for a moment.

'I hardly think there's much doubt about that.'

'And it's really him?' asked Ursula Brown, clutching the arm of the journalist.

The coldly scientific eye of the psychiatrist turned back to the corpse.

'Those are his clothes: the corduroy jacket, the tie, et cetera. And even though the face has been damaged considerably, those seem to be his features. So I would say that the body lying here is that of Gerry Pearson, beyond any reasonable doubt.'

'So he really has been murdered,' moaned Madge, who could not tear her eyes away from the victim.

'It's quite clear that a sword planted as deeply as that in the back rules out any question of accident or suicide. As for murder....' He looked around the room. 'Everyone will agree that no person made of human flesh and bone could have crossed the threshold of this door during the last hour, including Pearson himself: we found the seals intact and the door bolted from the inside by Pearson himself. The only other way in is through the window, which, although we found it open, is protected by that solid iron grill, which was intact. So how could our murderer have got in? And how, above all, could he have escaped? He wasn't here when we searched the place—and there's nowhere large enough to hide a human anyway. The chest, which only contains a few old wooden toys, is too small. And the chimney is not only too narrow, but is blocked by two metal bars.'

'Not to mention the sword,' added Hallahan, who was examining the window. 'It's the one in the stone. I recognised the mark I made, and so did Gail.' Blake nodded in agreement. 'What about you, Mr. Page?'

Bill approached the body, adjusted his spectacles to inspect the handle, straightened up and announced:

'No doubt whatsoever.'

'Aside from the Herculean force needed to pull the sword out of the stone, and the mystery of how the murderer got in and out of the room,' continued Hallahan, 'there's also the small problem of how the sword got into this sealed room.'

'I'm going to start by taking a look at the stone,' announced Gail Blake, going over to the door.

'Good idea, if only to find out what state it's in. Meanwhile, let's just think. We're all agreed the sword wasn't in the room when we searched, aren't we? My first thought was that it had been passed through the grill, but come over here and take a look. First of all, the grill is firmly anchored in the stone—there's no question of trickery. Now look at how it's made: dozens of diamond shapes of less than six inches each side. I haven't tried, but I'm pretty sure the guard of the sword is too wide to pass through.'

'It looks as though you're right,' said Dr. Jerrold, 'but we'll have to wait for the representatives of the law, unfortunately, before we can be sure.'

'That's just one more mystery,' sighed Hallahan, lowering his gaze. 'But, on top of all those physical impossibilities, there are psychological ones, even more strange if you ask me—But look there!'

'What is it?' asked Jerrold. 'The floor and the chest are a little wet? It's not surprising with all these winds and showers. Look at the window, it's banging all the time and is drenched by the rain.'

'That's not what I'm talking about. Something has disappeared from on top of the chest.'

'The Grail!' exclaimed Jerrold.

'Pearson placed it on the chest before we left, and it's gone. Add it to the list of mysteries.'

'In the legend he was talking about, he said it could float in the air,' added Ursula.

'In the legend, yes,' stressed Hallahan. 'There! We looked at the chest, but I can see something behind it.' He bent down and retrieved a piece of green material which he waved in the air. 'I recognise it: it's what he wrapped the Grail in. But I'm afraid it won't help us much.'

After nodding in agreement, Jerrold asked:

'What were you saying about psychological mysteries?'

'That they seemed even stranger than the physical ones. How could a sane man, knowing he was going to be murdered, comport himself the way he did, with the light-hearted excitement of someone participating in a game? Plus which, he seemed to go out of his way to help the killer carry out the project, namely his own murder.'

Hallahan paused, as if to add weight to his words:

'I don't know whether it's sunk in yet, but, as of now, his predictions have turned out to be true: he's been killed by use of the sword, and probably by one of us.'

'You mean, by me,' offered Ursula, coming forward. 'That's what he said, isn't it? That I would strike the fatal blow. Well, it hasn't worked out that way. I have a cast-iron alibi. During all but a couple of minutes of his last hour, I was with Frank. Frank, tell them it's true.'

The reporter nodded his head solemnly:

'It's perfectly true. It was around half past nine when I left here. I descended the tower, had a quick cigarette, and went to see Ursula. I swear that, from that time until the moment we heard the scream, she didn't leave my sight for a second. Did you hear me: not a single second.'

There was another silence, during which Dunbar, who seemed to expect a response, looked uncomfortable. He continued, almost aggressively:

'We left Pearson at nine-thirty and the scream occurred at ten-thirty, which left the murderer roughly an hour to do the deed. Who else has an alibi as strong as ours for that period?'

After the short explanations which followed, it transpired that nobody had, every one of the others having spent at least half an hour alone.

'There,' concluded Dunbar. 'If there's anyone not guilty, it's Ursula Brown!'

'You seem to be forgetting something,' observed Hallahan, picking up the piece of burnt material. 'It's exactly what Pearson predicted: *Ursula will contrive to have a perfect alibi, and prove the crime couldn't have been committed. At least physically.*

'Which is, you have to agree, precisely the situation we find ourselves in. I fear, my dear Dunbar, that your testimony, contrary to what you may think, doesn't help Ursula at all. And there's something else... Tell me, Miss Brown, at the start of the evening, just after we reached the courtyard, weren't you sporting a small, dark-coloured cloak, of a reddish hue?'

'A cloak? Yes, I put it on to go out. Why the question?'

'Where is it?'

'I don't know. Probably in my room.'

'Come and look at this charred cloth.'

Ursula Brown, suddenly pale, went over to join the white-bearded man. She bent down to look at the material, which was still smoking, then recoiled in shock:

'But it's not possible! It looks like my cloak.'

Hallahan nodded solemnly:

'That what I thought. I hope you can remember where and when you last saw it.'

Ursula's beautiful features went ashen. Her hands trembled and she seemed about to panic:

'My God, I don't know... Wait! Yes, I put it down when we came back to the lounge after looking at the sword in the stone. And it was only some time later that I realised it wasn't there any more. But I wasn't unduly worried, because I'm rather forgetful and I thought that maybe I'd left it somewhere else.'

A footfall on the stairs presaged the return of Blake who, somewhat breathless, appeared in the doorway.

'There's nothing there! The entire block of stone has vanished.'

Not a muscle of the historian's face moved as he replied:

'We're not going to find it any time soon. It was probably pushed over the cliff.'

'It would take a hell of a force to do that.'

'And even more to remove the sword,' retorted Hallahan. 'But let's leave it at that for the moment. Let's get back to the cloak, my dear "Morgan", which you offered to your brother, King Arthur.'

'But I never offered anything. And stop using those stupid nicknames.'

'I did it on purpose. Has no one made the connection between the flaming cloak and an episode in the Arthurian legend? Don't you remember Pearson saying Morgan le Fay, Arthur's sister, never stopped trying to do him harm?

'One day, a servant came to the king, bringing him a present of a beautiful cloak on behalf of her mistress, Morgan le Fay, to seek forgiveness for having played a dirty trick on him. But Arthur wasn't fooled and sensed a trap. He ordered the servant to put it on, whereupon she turned into a human torch. The connection is obvious: Pearson was burnt by a cloak belonging to Ursula, alias "Morgan le Fay."

'Let me remind you, Dunbar, that Miss Brown's alibi depends entirely on your word, and you must be aware that the knight Accolon, whom you represent, was madly in love with Morgan le Fay and ready to do anything for her.'

Stunned, the journalist shook his head:

'It's sheer madness.'

'You're quite right, of course,' sighed Hallahan, retuning to the body. 'It's all absurd and diabolically logical from beginning to end. It could all be a gigantic practical joke, were it not for the very real corpse lying here in front of us.'

Gail Blake, striking his forehead with the palm of his hand, added:

'Yes, it's all absurd, but what I absolutely refuse to accept is that this fellow Pearson killed himself—or let someone else kill him—for the sake of a practical joke. That's simply unthinkable. I know he had a twisted mind, but surely not to that point.'

'Suppose it wasn't him,' suggested Hallahan. 'Suppose the body isn't his? Don't ask me how he managed to get here, I couldn't tell you for the moment. I know, despite the burnt face, it does look like him but, the situation being what it is, we can't rule anything out. Come to think of it, Miss Pearson, didn't your uncle have a brother?'

Madge seemed stung to the quick.

'My father was his half-brother, but he's dead,' she retorted. 'And I might add they were not at all alike, physically or spiritually.'

'I wasn't talking about your father.'

'Wait,' she said pensively. 'Yes, of course, there was that other half-brother, Horatio, who spent much of his life in hospital. I never saw him, but I was told they resembled each other closely. My God! You don't mean to say that's him?'—she indicated the corpse—'and Uncle Gerry murdered him?'

'In your opinion, was he capable of it?'

'I—I don't know,' she stammered. 'That would be horrible. Heavens above!' she exclaimed suddenly, her face brightening, 'There's one way to find out.'

Everyone looked at Madge who, despite all that had happened, basked in the satisfaction of being the centre of attention, if only for a few moments.

'It's simple: Uncle Gerry had a port-wine birthmark on his right forearm. I noticed it earlier when I applied the ointment after he'd been burnt by an ember. We just need to check.'

Hallahan and Dr. Jerrold immediately set about rolling up the dead man's sleeve as carefully as possible. Madge and the other occupants of the room held their breath. The appearance of the birthmark, immediately confirmed by Madge, was not a cause for relief. Quite the contrary.

'We're back to where we started,' sighed Blake.

Hallahan started to pace back and forth in front of the fire, which was dwindling in the grate.

'Wait!' he said suddenly. 'It's meaningless. I thought there was something odd about the business of being burned by an ember. Tell me, Miss Pearson, did you actually see the burn with your own eyes?'

'Well, no, not really.'

'So he could very well have made up the incident so you would see the so-called birthmark, which he could have created himself somehow. A birthmark similar to the real one on our corpse here.'

One could have heard a pin drop.

'I have a feeling we're going round in circles,' declared Dr. Jerrold, with the flicker of a smile.

'Wait! I think we've forgotten someone,' interjected Bill suddenly. 'Someone who knows your uncle well, Madge, and who could help us: Peter Cobb, the guard and handyman.'

'My goodness, of course!' exclaimed Madge. 'The poor man, he must still be in his hut in this foul weather.'

'I think we need to talk to him,' suggested Bill who, with general agreement, went to find him.

The little group decided to return to the lounge, where they partook of a welcome cordial. It was decided that someone should go to alert the police, once Bill and Peter Cobb returned. At that point, Gail Blake started to talk. He seemed embarrassed and his tone was serious.

'I don't know which way to turn, with everything that's happened. Everything's going too fast. As I told you earlier, during that hour's wait, I'd gone to stand guard near the tower. Not inside the courtyard like you, Jerrold, but outside, to the north-west. I'd left the castle by the entrance, following a dangerously rocky path, to reach a point where, to be frank, I couldn't see very much. I spent more time trying not to lose my balance than watching the famous tower. The ocean was rumbling down below and it was raining so heavily as to make my testimony questionable. From where I was standing I could only see the north angle of the tower and not the western section, which contained the window of the room where Pearson had installed himself. I could just discern a halo of light at that level. Well, whether you believe me or not, it seemed to me that something was moving along the angle of the wall, as if someone was climbing up that side.'

Hallahan looked at his friend dubiously:

'As far as I can make out, Gail, it's almost impossible to scale any of the walls of the tower, particularly on that side.'

'I know, that's why I say my testimony has to be taken with a pinch of salt.'

'Suppose it's him?' stammered Madge in a faint voice. '*Him...* King Arthur!'

The history professor nodded slowly and declared in a solemn voice:

'He's fit and well on Avalon and ready to return if the mood takes him. He's slumbering on Avalon, awaiting the hour of vengeance.'

'Please stop!' screamed the young woman. 'Do you want us all to die of fear?'

'I'm only repeating your uncle's words.'

At that moment, the bell at the front entrance rang insistently.

The guests looked at each other in surprise

'It must be Bill,' murmured Madge who, like the others, wondered why he bothered to announce his return.

Gail Blake left the lounge and returned quickly with two men who were neither Bill Page nor Peter Cobb. The two of them, one a tall, lugubrious individual in police uniform, and the other, a man of medium height with an inquisitive look and wearing a dark raincoat, seemed to be part of a team. The man in the raincoat introduced himself brusquely:

'Inspector Roy of the Bodmin police. This is Sergeant Hunt. We've received a telegram announcing a murder in the castle, for tonight.'

9

'We already know what happened here,' said Inspector Roy. 'We met Mr. Page on our way up.'

'Bill? Then why isn't he here?' asked Madge, shivering.

She didn't like this dry-as-dust inspector. His bushy eyebrows and black beard, while not as impressive as Gail Blake's, gave him a cold severity he didn't need. The beanpole Hunt, he of the funereal demeanour, seemed almost pleasant by comparison.

'After what he told us,' replied the policeman, 'I immediately sent him to get reinforcements from the police station in Tincastle.'

'On foot? In this weather?' asked Madge anxiously.

'There's no other way to get there, miss. It's not all that far, anyway. In any case, we didn't have much choice. Our presence here—Sergeant Hunt and myself—seemed to be urgent and imperative.'

'But couldn't Peter Cobb have gone instead?'

'If you're speaking of the young man guarding the entrance to the castle, I ordered him not to leave his post. His testimony could be determinant, as it appears that no one can get in or out of the castle without him seeing them. Can someone show us to the scene of the crime?'

While Blake and Dunbar stayed with Madge and Ursula, Dr. Jerrold and Josiah Hallahan accompanied the police officers while describing the events of the night. The inspector listened without saying a word. Once at the scene of the crime, he paid particular attention to the window. He also sniffed what was left of the burnt cape and detected the odour of methylated spirits. Next, he examined the body and the sword, remarking to his subordinate that there were no fingerprints on the latter. After a reflective pause, he withdrew the sword from the corpse, wiped the tip, and examined it carefully to assure himself of its solidity. He asked Sergeant Hunt to do the same, then Hallahan and Jerrold, somewhat to their surprise. The psychiatrist's inspection was cursory, and he got rid of the weapon as if it were red-hot. As for the history professor, he was more meticulous and even severe with the blade, which he tried to bend in different positions, but with the same result. Inspector Roy took the sword, went over to the window, and thrust the blade through one of the lozenges, where the guard blocked it.

His normally impassive features wore a frustrated expression.

'I already thought of that,' observed Hallahan. 'The killer, from outside, drove the weapon through the iron grill and into the victim's back. Setting aside how he managed to climb the tower and how he got the victim to turn his back to the window, it seemed at the time like the only possible solution....'

'Which we can now definitely rule out. It's only a matter of an inch or so, but the guard won't go through and it can't be bent. Pity.'

The room was once again searched from top to bottom, and with the same result: no secret passage or hiding-place. All four men went down to the little courtyard and out through the postern gate leading to the plateau where the sword had been impaled in the stone. Thanks to his powerful torchlight, the inspector was able to discern tracks on the rocky surface leading to the edge of the cliff, suggesting the stone had been displaced.

'It was shoved into the sea,' he observed. 'No point in worrying about it for the moment. We'll have to look at it in the light of day, which won't be easy with those reefs and waves. You say the sword was solidly embedded in the stone?'

'Yes, with mortar, I think,' replied Hallahan. 'But I really can't see how it was removed, without equipment and in so short a time. The only explanation I can see is that the stone was pushed into the sea—which obviously did happen—and then the sword was recovered afterwards. But take a look down there, if you have the courage to get close enough to the edge. With those reefs and the raging sea, it's absolutely impossible.'

The climb up the tower, particularly on the north and west sides, seemed just as impossible. True, the rocky surface was far from smooth, but it was out of the question to climb up the sheer vertical faces. As for reaching the window from the roof, the latter was every bit as inaccessible as the former. And climbing up with the help of a rope implied the help of the victim to attach it to the iron grill.

'But even if that were true,' growled the inspector, 'what would our daring acrobat have done, clinging onto the rope, buffeted by the wind, with a sheer drop onto those menacing rocks and the risk of being swallowed up by the raging sea? No, that seems just as insane as everything else. Let's go back inside. We can look at all this later when the reinforcements arrive. Hunt, you go back to the scene of the crime to guard the body and look for more clues.'

Once back in the lounge, Inspector Roy decided to take stock of the situation, while waiting for the local police to arrive.

'I've an important statement to make, which will probably surprise all of you. But before I do so, I'm going to go over the main facts about this murder, which is an unusual one, to say the least.

'Let's start at the beginning: you all received an invitation on some vague pretext, but sufficiently intriguing to lure you all here. We don't know if any others were also invited.

'For starters, so to speak, Pearson announces there's going to be a murder. During the meal, he makes a few vague accusations and gives each of you a name from the Arthurian legends. Things are going swimmingly when he announces his second surprise: he will be the victim.

'And that's not the end of it. That would be too simple. He shows you the weapon, gets you to admit you can't remove it, then asks some of you to mark it with a distinctive sign, so it may be formally identified later. Then he announces the name of his prospective killer and explains that she will have a cast-iron alibi, which will mean she can't be materially accused of the crime. By the way, it's lucky the police don't have to deal with this situation every day, or we'd be faced with people confessing to crimes just for the sake of appearing innocent.

'At this point, everything seems too far-fetched to be taken seriously. The aforementioned Pearson allows himself to be incarcerated in a sealed room, bolted from the inside for good measure, where he's found an hour later, after having uttered a cry of distress. Was it really he who cried out? I doubt it. If we could know the precise moment of death... what do you think, doctor? You examined the body immediately after the cry, in other words around ten-thirty.'

The psychiatrist didn't reply immediately. He had seemed thoughtful for a while already.

'Sorry. Were you asking about the time of death? The body was still warm, so I believe death occurred no more than half an hour earlier. Only an autopsy will tell more precisely. But, in view of the severity of the wound, I think it highly unlikely he could have cried out. That's just a personal opinion, in the absence of other evidence.'

'I came to the same conclusion,' agreed the inspector, 'but let's continue. The first remarkable thing is the absolute impossibility of a human being to have committed this crime. The door, the chimney and the window were all sealed. We thought we saw a faint glimmer of hope regarding the window, but that was quickly extinguished, because the whole sword couldn't have passed through the iron grill. No secret passage, either. Suicide, accident. Ruled out by general agreement. The second remarkable thing is the weapon: the famous "sword of King Arthur" which, not content with being pulled out of its rock, turns up in this sealed room to plant itself between the shoulders of the victim. How? By what process? Mystery... The only thing we can say for sure about the murderer is that he wore gloves, because he didn't leave a single fingerprint on the pommel of the sword. As for the Grail, the cup which Pearson took into the room with him to conjure up the evil spirit, I can guarantee you it's not there anymore. There's one final point: the famous cloak wrapped in flames around the victim's head. It's a significant detail.'

Ursula stood up, her face crimson:

'Is that an accusation?'

Inspector Roy shook his head:

'Not at all. That cloak has a particular importance, but not in the sense you think. I'm not going to dwell on the time or the manner it was taken from you. There was too much going on to hope for a clue in that direction. The cloak, light enough at the outset, was drenched in methylated spirits. It was a deliberate effort to render the deceased's features unrecognisable. Which brings me to the important statement I have to make....'

The policeman took several steps forward, a vague smile on his lips, so as to prolong the anticipation of his audience. He continued, addressing his words to Madge in particular:

'The body cannot be that of your uncle, Miss Pearson... No more than the man who welcomed you and pretended to be your uncle can really be him. Because Gerry Pearson... *has been dead for a year.*'

10

Before the eyes of his flabbergasted audience, Inspector Roy, clearly pleased with the consternation he had caused, put two new logs on the fire and riddled the hearth assiduously. He turned suddenly and gave Madge a searching look:

'How long is it since you last saw your uncle, miss?'

Madge, still bewildered and in a state of shock, stammered:

'About twelve years. I was nine or ten at the time. I... It's true, when I saw him again this evening, I thought he'd changed a lot: he looked quite a bit older. In fact I recognised him by the way he behaved and the way he looked at me.'

The inspector turned to the psychiatrist, with an enquiring look.

'It's quite simple,' said Jerrold. 'I never spoke to him before coming here.'

Professor Hallahan stroked his white beard thoughtfully:

'I'd met him at some conference or other, but he was only a nodding acquaintance. We had a lively discussion once about some historic detail or other, but that was quite a while ago. The last time I saw him must have been at least two years ago. When I saw the man who passed himself off as Pearson, I said to myself he'd changed a lot, but I put that down to aging, without thinking any more about it.'

'It's pretty well the same for me,' said Gail Blake, nodding slowly. 'I knew him without knowing him. The last time I saw him goes back a good two years. He certainly wasn't a close friend—far from it. We'd already spoken, but only to hurl insults at each other across pub tables or from the gallery to the auditorium in those famous Celtic conferences. I found he'd changed a lot as well.'

'As for me,' declared Frank Dunbar, with a malicious look in his eye, 'I'd heard a lot about him, but I'd never met him. Lucky for him, I have to say. By the way, what did he die of?'

The policeman cleared his throat before replying:

'A natural death. A stroke, I believe. I hadn't got time to do a detailed investigation: I only received the telegram this evening. I just had time to phone a colleague before we had to leave.'

He turned to Ursula Brown:

'How about you, Miss Brown? As far as I can make out, you knew him better than anyone else here.'

Ursula thought for a moment, then answered in a calm, detached voice:

'About twenty years ago, I lived with him—here, in fact—for three months. I knew him very well… too well, I might add.'

The inspector stroked his chin:

'It's rather curious, then, that you didn't spot the deception.'

'Twenty years is a long time,' retorted Ursula. 'But there's another reason. He played his part very well, because he seemed able to read me like an open book—just like Gerry.'

'I believe I understand,' interjected Dr. Jerrold, in an awkwardly respectful voice. 'When you almost went off the cliff, it wasn't because of a stick, was it?'

Ursula nodded silently.

'I noticed it,' continued the psychiatrist, 'because my profession requires a keen sense of observation and because I'm used to such cases. I had a patient once who made an obsession out of this benign infirmity to the point of refusing to leave the house. His myopia was complicated by agoraphobia, a considerably more disturbing affliction. It's important to note that the patient, in such cases, given the human condition, be—.'

'So you're short–sighted,' cut in the policeman, looking at the young woman.

Ursula hung her head.

'Yes, but I prefer not to wear glasses, just the same.'

Frank Dunbar, who had just served himself another glass of champagne, commented out loud about the mysteries of the female psyche and how an aesthetic concern almost cost the woman her life.

'Getting back to that man,' continued Ursula, 'as I was saying, he was a clever actor who knew a lot of things about us.'

'There's not much doubt about that,' replied the inspector. 'But I fear that, despite new information, we are far from determining the obscure plans of this individual. We don't even know if it was he who was murdered. Everything we've learned is so twisted and complex that the theory of the port-wine birthmark, put forward by one of you, seems quite probable. But before we jump to any conclusions about the ambiguous role of this *deus ex machina*, I propose we take a look at the rest of the premises. We may well find a few useful clues.'

Madge, Ursula and Dunbar remained in the lounge to await the return of Bill with the local police. The inspection of the second floor, composed essentially of guest rooms, was brief and fruitless. The first floor was scarcely furnished and in a state of near abandon, with the exception of a room containing three wardrobes full of material and a dressing-table with three mirrors. Crammed with cosmetic products and make-up accessories, it would not have been out of place in a theatre, as the inspector observed.

'All this stinks of a stage production,' he commented, foraging through the items on the marble top. 'What do you think?'

Hallahan and Blake nodded, as did Dr. Jerrold, who was looking more and more thoughtful:

'There's something in the back of my mind. Something I can't put my finger on. My memory is playing me tricks.'

'Haven't you got a colleague who specialises in this sort of thing?' asked Blake, trying to keep a straight face.

The psychiatrist pretended not to have heard.

'My little finger tells me it's something important.'

'Your little finger?' repeated Blake. 'You're talking like one of your patients.'

'At the moment, I am a patient, otherwise I would already have answered my own question.'

'Let's get on with it,' cut in the policeman curtly. 'Let's look at the cellar.'

The library, not far from the lounge, attracted their attention briefly. Madge had joined them at the inspector's request. The shelves were stacked with old books and others of a particular orientation.

'Several copies of Geoffrey of Monmouth's *History of the Kings of Britain,*' said Josiah Hallahan, with a connoisseur's appreciation. 'Several works by the great Chrétien de Troyes, to whom we owe our beloved Lancelot. Walter Scott, of course and the collected works of Markale—.'

'And quite a few detective novels,' Blake noted. 'With a predilection for Edgar Allan Poe.'

'I remember,' said Madge. 'Uncle Gerry adored his work. He would often read me one of his tales in the evening, after which I could never get to sleep. He liked anything to do with the supernatural or witchcraft.'

'That's pretty obvious,' replied Inspector Roy, running his finger along the dusty covers. 'But it's nevertheless strange: we know this man wasn't your uncle, Miss Pearson, yet the macabre comedy he created was entirely in keeping with your uncle's spirit. The Arthurian staging, to mention but one aspect....'

Once again, Madge found herself in the grip of an emotional crisis.

She looked around. She remembered only too well the dusty old bookcase full of books on magic. Uncle Gerry had spoken about it as if it were a holy sanctuary, full of mysteries and frightening images. He locked it carefully, yet showed ostensibly where the key was hidden. As soon as his back was turned, Madge took advantage in order to visit the sanctuary, torn between curiosity and fear, avidly searching for treatises on witchcraft with mysterious etchings, so terrifying for the young girl that she was at the time.

So Uncle Gerry was dead? Perhaps. But she sensed he was still there, almost close to her, behind those walls of books which so impassioned her.

Immediately thereafter, she followed the four men into the cellar. Unlike them, she was not interested in the tools and other objects in a small workshop they found at the end of a corridor with a vaulted ceiling.

'Pretty well equipped,' observed the inspector, after foraging in all four corners. 'Mind you, if you're all on your own in such a place, you need to be ready for the unexpected. Plumbing wrenches, tools for tapping and threading, nothing's been left out. There's even a pillar drill.' He drew the attention of the other three to the metal shavings scattered on the work-bench. 'And it looks as though someone has used it recently. What do you think, gentlemen?'

Madge took advantage of the men's preoccupation to tiptoe away. She felt drained. If only Bill were there with her. She was starting to worry about how long he'd been away. It was now well past midnight and he was still not back. She estimated it was possible to get to the village in half an hour, if one hurried. Add the time it took to alert the police, plus the return trip....

After checking with Ursula and Dunbar that he still hadn't returned, she decided to go outside, despite a wind that was gathering strength.

Once the idea of going to meet Bill occurred to her, she knew she couldn't wait any longer. A plague on that sinister Inspector Roy! She didn't need to ask his permission. What's more, she'd see Peter Cobb on the way, and she was sure he'd welcome the opportunity to chat with someone.

She left the castle by a postern gate the other guests didn't know about, which led to a steep path which led in a roundabout way to a point near Peter's hut.

"Peter's still there," she told herself when she saw there was a light in the window of the little hut. She found that comforting as she moved forward, the thundering sounds of the sea below bringing back memories of the many hours of sheer terror she had spent in that very place during her childhood.

The painful recollections seemed like a bad dream, a nightmare which she was reliving while wide awake.

What could she make of the last few hours? Those insane events which *couldn't* have taken place, but which she had witnessed with her own eyes. Who was the impostor who had played the part of her uncle? Why hadn't she been informed of his death the year before? Was it his body which had been found in the sealed room? How had he been killed? Apparently, only a ghost could have committed the crime. But whose ghost? King Arthur's? She remembered the words of the impostor: *"He's awaiting the hour of vengeance...."*

Lost in thought, she suddenly fancied she heard a noise close by. She stopped, but could hear nothing above the persistent wind. Approaching the hut, she was surprised not to see the gatekeeper's shadow through the window. She called out, knocked on the door and, not receiving a response, went in.

There was nobody there. The place was skimpily furnished: a chair, some shelves, and a table with an oil lamp. A packet of cigarettes, an empty ashtray and a small jug of coffee. That was all. Peter was noticeable by his absence.

Madge tried to gather her thoughts. In vain. Peter's desertion seemed a bad sign. She went out, hesitated a moment on the doorstep, then—instead of taking the path back to the castle—started down towards the little bridge. After a few yards, she heard someone call out:

'Miss! Miss!'

It sounded like Peter's voice. She turned round, looked up and saw a figure far above her, near the highest point on the island. Peter was running towards her with great bounds, frantically calling her name. She went to meet him, and it was a breathless and haggard Peter who stood before her.

'I saw him, I saw him with my own eyes. With his long red cloak and his sword.'

'Who the devil are you talking about?'

'*Him*. King Arthur. He killed that man with his sword, up there on the edge of the cliff, and then disappeared as if by magic!'

11

Madge felt as though she were losing her mind. She stared blindly at Peter for a few seconds while, in her mind's eye, a procession of knights in armour galloped before her, led by their brave sovereign, Arthur.

King Arthur? No, Peter couldn't have seen any such thing. The solitude, the waiting, the fatigue... he must have drifted off for a few minutes and started to dream.

She started to reason with him, but Peter wasn't listening:

'I couldn't do anything, do you understand? Nothing! When he raised his sword it was too late. I called out, I shouted... all in vain. How could he have heard me anyway, up there, with all that wind?'

'Peter!' shouted Madge, who felt she was about to lose her grip, 'what in heaven's name are you talking about?'

'I don't know! I wasn't close enough to see clearly. I was there, in the hut, thinking to myself that, if I didn't get up and walk around a bit, my legs would go to sleep. I went out, and that's when I saw him running around on the plateau at the top of the island as if someone was after him. I shouted out, but he couldn't hear me.'

An icy shiver ran up Madge's spine: suppose it was Bill?

'It seemed really strange, especially after what I'd been told and the arrival of those two policemen. So, I decided to take a look up there. Do you know it? Compared to here, it's quite flat and it's easy to get your bearings. There's a promontory up there on the same side of the island as the castle, which is lower down, and on it there's a row of large rocks. One of the rocks hides the entrance to a grotto. It's the highest point on the island, and it's the most dangerous: one false step and goodbye.

'That's the direction he seemed to be headed, and that's the direction I took to go after him. Carefully, because there are sudden squalls of rain which can catch you off balance. That's when I saw him again, near the entrance to the grotto. He seemed very agitated, as if he was looking for an escape route and he got really close to the edge. That's when *the other one* sprang out of the grotto.'

Peter swallowed before continuing:

'I could only see vague shapes at that distance, but the newcomer had a long cloak which flapped in the wind and a big sword. And there was something majestic about him, if you know what I mean. When he watched the other without revealing his presence and especially when he raised his sword, that's when I understood.

'I shouted out, but it was too late. The sword came down two, three, four times, I lost count. And that's when something incredible happened: *the murderer disappeared.*

'I know, the wind and the rain blinded me, it was very dark, and under such conditions, someone crouching behind a rock could have given the same impression. But it's not possible. I went up to see. There was definitely someone lying on the ground, but the other one had vanished. There's no hiding-place up there, do you understand, unless you throw yourself over the edge! And he was too far away from the grotto to have gone back there without me seeing.'

'And you didn't see who the victim was?' asked Madge in a strangled voice.

'No, it was dangerous enough as it was. The "knight" could have reappeared at any moment. I think the victim was wearing a dark coat, that's all I can tell you. Somebody needs to be there on the spot. Go and warn the others. I have to stay here, the inspector told me not to budge.'

Madge didn't need to be asked twice. Ten minutes later, in the castle lounge with everyone present, she went over what Peter had told her.

'We need to get there as quickly as possible,' she concluded breathlessly. 'It could be Bill.'

'Yes, there's not a minute to lose,' agreed Blake, who seemed to be losing some of his masculine assurance. 'It's funny, now you mention a cloak flapping, it seems to me that's what I saw: that shape standing out from the side of the tower and moving steadily upwards.'

'It's extraordinary,' said Josiah Hallahan, who seemed both terrified and entranced. 'So, *he's* returned from magical Avalon.'

'Yes, but with evil intent,' thundered Blake.

'Everyone betrayed him, Gail. Do you remember?'

'So, let's go.' Blake looked at Madge, who was casting her eye round the room in bewilderment. 'What is it, miss? What are you looking for?'

'Inspector Roy isn't here with you?'

'He went to meet his colleague, just after you left. But—that's curious—he should be back by now: he said he'd only be a few minutes. They've probably found a new clue. In any case, they need to be notified. I'll go.'

Madge, exhausted and a bundle of nerves, collapsed on the throne. So much happening in such a short period of time. The clock showed five minutes to one; the hands seemed to slow down as the events accelerated. Fortunately for her, she had no idea of what the rest of the night would bring.

The fire crackled quietly next to her, and she allowed herself to relax in the comfort of its agreeable heat. The people she saw in front of her were out of place in the medieval décor—their clothes, at least. That Ursula Brown, with her long, silky red tresses, would have made a beautiful princess. Beautiful but evil. The nickname "Morgan le Fay" fit her like a glove. Suppose she was the murderer? So far, everything the man who impersonated her uncle had said, had actually happened. What's more, as had become glaringly obvious, her alibi didn't hold up. That Frank Dunbar was obviously under her thumb and, as a consequence, his testimony was worthless. "Morgan le Fay"? She was that, assuredly. You only needed to look into her eyes to become convinced of that. As for Dr. Jerrold, he was perfect in the part of Mordred, the traitor. He was polite, with excellent manners, but she wouldn't have wanted him as her doctor. Something about him gave her the chills. Maybe it was his eyes, like two unpolished stones.

He came over to her and cleared his throat before speaking:

'You told us a while ago that you'd never met your uncle's brother, did you not?'

'His half-brother,' replied Madge, correcting him. 'No I never saw him.'

'Was he slightly older?'

'Yes, obviously, because he was the first born on his mother's side. But only by two or three years. He looked like Uncle Gerry, apparently. Is that what you wanted to know?'

'We talked about it just now, Blake and Hallahan and I. Why didn't you think of the brother as the impersonator of your uncle?'

Madge shrugged her shoulders:

'If he was, he's dead now. Somebody killed him. Somebody who's just committed a second crime.'

At that moment, Gail Blake burst into the room. His previous calm assurance had left him. He announced, gabbling his words:

'I couldn't find the inspector. Or Sergeant Hunt. And there's something else: the body's disappeared. It's no longer in the room at the top of the tower.'

There was a deathly silence.

'I suggest,' continued Blake, 'that some of us stay here and try to find the police, and the others take a look at the new victim.'

Ursula Brown and Madge, the only ones to know the island well, were chosen to go to the scene of the new crime, together with Blake, the poet, and Dunbar, the journalist. Madge led them through the postern gate she had used a short while before. After having zig-zagged a few yards between some rocks, she took them up a steep slope which led to the summit of the island, where the wind seemed to double its intensity. The sea was scarcely visible, but it made its presence felt, and powerfully so. It could be heard rumbling while it assaulted the island, and seemed to have decided to engulf it. That, at least, was the impression Madge had when the four of them reached the famous promontory.

It was, in fact, a very dangerous place. Blake and Dunbar, who were both in unfamiliar territory, were obviously nervous. The rocks were slippery and they wobbled in the gusts of wind. When the light of a lamp revealed a body lying near the edge of the promontory, Madge's heart skipped a beat. She breathed a sigh of relief when she realised it wasn't Bill: she recognised the uniform of Sergeant Hunt.

'Well,' growled Blake, 'it seems that Peter wasn't dreaming. It's Hunt, there's no doubt about it. A massive blow to the head, probably by a sword, and surely by the same one, because I didn't see it in the room.'

Sergeant Hunt lay stretched out on the stony ground. He wasn't wearing a helmet and it was probably for that reason, thought Madge, that Peter hadn't recognised the policeman. The blood seeping from the wound had spattered his hair and was now—diluted by the rain—running down his right cheek to a lower lip curled in a sinister rictus, before dribbling down onto the rocky ground. Two rents in his coat at shoulder level indicated he had received other blows, but no one felt like subjecting the body to further examination.

The sight of the corpse in such a dangerous spot and the fantastic décor straight out of a fairy tale shook them badly, and they were all anxious to leave, but not before examining the small grotto—about six feet wide and as much deep—which failed to yield any clues. They also tried to evoke the scene described by Peter, and concluded that the only way the assailant could have avoided being seen by him was to have thrown himself into the reef-strewn sea.

They returned to the castle haggard, exhausted and drenched to the skin. In the lounge, Josiah Hallahan informed them that the reinforcements had still not arrived and Inspector Roy was nowhere to be found.

'Something must have happened to Bill on the way, otherwise he would have been back by now,' moaned Madge, warming herself by the fire.

Blake looked up at the clock:

'Not necessarily. Don't forget he was travelling at night. However, I don't think I'll be able to sit here waiting, what with the policeman who's disappeared and these two corpses. Excuse me: this corpse. The other one's disappeared.'

'I'm going to look for him,' announced Madge suddenly, with a firmness which brooked no dissent.

None of those present, shaken to the core by the confirmation of a second murder, raised any objection. Blake seemed to have recovered his courage and proposed accompanying her, arguing that she faced great danger going out alone, and he had no desire to have to look for a third dead body on the cliff edges.

Madge left the castle with a determined step, which Blake was hard-pressed to follow. The first surprise awaited them at the watchman's hut. Once again, there was a light in the window but no shadow. After exchanging bewildered glances, they went inside. Nobody. But on the table, Madge could see a scrap of paper pinned beneath the ashtray. A hasty hand had scrawled a note:

Gone to village. Too many strange things here. Peter.

'Too many strange things here?' repeated Blake. 'That's certainly true, but what does it mean? Did something new happen which was the last straw? What do you think? It seems bizarre.'

'Everything seems bizarre,' sighed Madge. 'And that's an understatement. Particularly since the last thing he said was he was going to stay at his post. Anyway, let's get going. There's no point in staying here.'

She crossed the little wooden bridge which sat on the old stone arch over the sea. Her heart was pounding. She was getting breathless from the fast pace she had set herself, but she was also driven by fear. Fear for Bill, who could quite easily have slipped anywhere along the dangerous path she and Blake were on at the moment. And fear for herself, for the sea—now much higher than when she traversed the bridge earlier—seemed to be lying in wait for the unwary, ready to wash them away with an enormous breaker into a watery grave. The waves crashing on the reefs below threw clouds of spray over her when they were not licking at her feet, and around her everywhere was the hellish noise, even more frightening because she could scarcely see anything at all.

They pressed forward as fast as they could safely go and eventually arrived at the village of Tincastle, where the sky and the elements seemed less inclement. The moon had broken through the clouds and was clearly visible behind the church steeple. The baleful light gave the old slate roofs and crooked gables a medieval aspect, heightened by the eerie silence, which prompted Madge once again to wonder whether she was living a bad dream. She was very happy to have the beefy Blake by her side, whose heavy step resounded noisily in the narrow streets. They searched in vain for a police station when suddenly, as they were nearing the town hall, a figure emerged from another street.

'Bill!' Madge cried, throwing discretion to the wind.

Bill it was. A few seconds later, she was in his arms. But the romantic aspect of their reunion did not last long. Bill was perspiring heavily and obviously agitated.

'It's insane, Madge,' he stammered, wiping his brow. 'There's no police station in this godforsaken village. There was one here last year, but it was closed down. I ran all over the place before I found out.'

'We've got a few things to tell you, young man,' announced Gail Blake solemnly, and proceeded to give him a brief summary of the latest events.

Flabbergasted, Bill remained speechless for some time.

'Well, there's no longer any doubt,' he said finally, with a sombre air.

'No doubt? Doubt about what?' asked Blake.

'As I told you, I searched for a long time for the police station. In vain. So I went to the town hall. I rang and I knocked, but there was no answer. Eventually I had to resort to waking people up. The first one sent me packing with a flea in my ear. The second one, who wore a nightcap, told me in no uncertain words there was no police station in Tincastle, but if people like me went roaming the streets at night, the matter would be taken up at the next council meeting. I fared a little better after that: an old woman told me the police station had been closed, and she knew that because her late husband had been a policeman. He'd died six months ago. As luck would have it, he'd been stationed in Bodmin, where Inspector Roy said he was based.'

Bill took off his glasses before continuing:

'When the woman told me she'd never heard her husband—who was very voluble on the subject of his colleagues—speak of an Inspector Roy, I thought maybe he'd been moved there recently. I thought also that he might have been mistaken about the death of your uncle, Madge... Ah, but I was forgetting: she also told me Uncle Gerry was alive and well. She saw him regularly when he came to do his shopping, and, in fact, she'd seen him only last week! I told myself the inspector had been misinformed, but now that he's disappeared, it's no longer in doubt: *we've been dealing with an impostor.*'

12

'An impostor,' repeated Blake, tugging angrily at his black beard. 'But, of course. Why didn't I think of that before? There were a number of odd things about his behaviour. The sword, for example, which he suddenly yanked out of the body without waiting for a specialist to perform an examination; and declaring, just by looking at it with the naked eye, that there were no fingerprints on it. No real police officer would have done that.'

'There was also his over-familiar manner,' said Madge. 'He put the logs on the fire as if he was at home. And I noticed that, for a stranger, he found his way around the castle very easily.'

'He tricked us. But what's surprising—.'

Blake never finished his sentence. A shutter was flung violently open behind him, and a masculine-looking woman with a pallid complexion and wearing a white nightgown looked out. She didn't mince her words, castigating the kind of people who prevent those who have to work the next day from sleeping. Blake used all his eloquence to calm the virago down with—to Madge's surprise—an amiable politeness which allowed him to question her about Gerry Pearson. She didn't appear to think much of the latter, but she did confirm what Bill had already learnt: he had been alive and well the week before.

'What are we going to do?' asked Madge anxiously, pressing herself against Bill. 'I don't understand anything anymore. Uncle Gerry is still alive? So was it he who greeted us after all? And the body, the one in the tower, is it his? And what role was the pretend Inspector Roy playing? Was it he who murdered his own colleague, Sergeant Hunt?'

'If Inspector Roy was a fake policeman, there's a good chance the sergeant was too,' observed Blake. 'We're standing here debating in the midst of utter insanity. I'm wondering what we should do now. Contact the police? Yes, but how? The nearest village is quite a long way away. On foot, in this weather, I think we should wait until it's light.'

'They wouldn't believe us here, if we tried to tell them our story,' said Bill, his eye on one of the nearby houses. 'We have to warn the others immediately. Who's to say whether the false Inspector Roy has left the island?'

'I see what you're saying,' agreed Blake with a nod of the head. 'We have no idea what the fellow's plans are, which could be very dangerous. We looked all over the castle for him, but it was a piece of cake for him to hide. As for the rest of the island....'

'The wisest thing to do would be to wait for daylight, and stick together.'

'You're right, young man,' acknowledged Blake. 'There's strength in numbers. But let's not waste time, let's go back to the castle and warn our friends, in the hope that nothing else happens to them.'

By a quarter to three, they were all together in the lounge once more. The news of Inspector Roy's deception and his lie about Pearson's death rocked them all back on their heels, and their faces expressed varying degrees of shock.

'It's not even three o'clock in the morning and so much has happened already,' said Bill, who had traded his sodden clothes for a tweed suit which, in Madge's opinion, gave him a stuffy air and made him look older.

He turned towards Madge but avoided her eye:

'I don't want you to think that I've got any preconceived ideas about your uncle, Madge, but we have to face the facts....'

'You're talking as though I've been defending him!'

'Very well, let me set the ball rolling. We now know, since he's not dead, that it was he who greeted us tonight. We're all aware of his peculiar character and twisted mind. Plus which—and this is well known—he's a lover of epic tales, well versed in the legends of the Knights of the Round Table, and an avid reader of detective fiction and anything which touches on occult science. So far, so good. If there's one thing that's indisputable, it's the theatrical nature of the events we've lived through so far: weird, extravagant and shocking, to say the least—not to mention macabre. It's been a grotesque comedy, not following any logic except that of Gerry Pearson's own twisted mind.'

'What you say is largely true,' agreed Josiah Hallahan, 'but I fear your judgment of Gerry Pearson is a little harsh.'

'Possibly. But let's assume for the sake of argument that boredom, solitude and God know what else aggravated his natural inclinations, and that he was the instigator of this Machiavellian scenario. Didn't he emphasize his noble roots? He practically vaunted himself as the direct descendant of Arthur himself. Moreover, when he was asked whether he would play the role of the king, he didn't pronounce one way or the other. Yes, he would be King Arthur: forlorn, betrayed, surrounded by enemies and, to cap it all, victim of a conspiracy. But he also spoke of *the other*, the one who would come in vengeance.'

'And who has already struck,' said Frank Dunbar, vehemently. 'You haven't seen Sergeant Hunt's body yet, up there. And are you aware of the circumstances of the murder?'

'Yes, I was told about it,' replied Bill, taken aback by the reporter's aggressive tone. 'But let me continue... I believe the port-wine birthmark on Pearson's forearm was a fake which he deliberately let Madge see, in order to fool us all and throw us off the scent; for it seems generally accepted that the body, despite a resemblance to Pearson, wasn't actually his. So, in that case, where did he go?

'Then suddenly, out of the blue, a self-proclaimed police inspector appears and immediately sends me down to the village in search of a police station which doesn't exist and a lot of other nonsense. The inspector seems to be in his forties, like Pearson, and the same height, but he's bearded and has thick eyebrows.'

'I see!' exclaimed Dunbar. 'The inspector was none other than Pearson himself!'

'It's highly likely,' replied Bill, looking at the astonished faces around him. 'It's also likely that the so-called Sergeant Hunt who accompanied him was an unwitting accomplice whom he had easily fooled—for the fellow didn't strike me as being particularly bright.'

'More to the point,' retorted Dunbar, '*how* did he kill him? That's the question. The murderer was seen this time, *yet he literally faded into the night.*'

'This is no time to start believing in ghosts,' replied Bill, adjusting his glasses. 'I know it's all very mysterious, but we need to look at things logically if we're going to get to the bottom of it. The so-called Sergeant Hunt was certainly killed because he was a witness, that's the essence of it. As to the how and wherefore, we'll come back to that when we know more. Now we come to the corpse in the tower....'

'Killed in a sealed room locked on the inside,' sneered the journalist, 'and with a sword which couldn't have been removed. Mere details.'

'All in good time. The important thing right now is to identify the body, which has so mysteriously vanished. Then find the reason for the murder. Everything's so twisted one's tempted to wonder if there is one. But it's one of the few things we have to go on.'

Nobody said a word, but there seemed to be general agreement. Madge never took her eyes off her fiancé, torn between her growing admiration for him—she had never seen him so confident—and her growing fear for her uncle.

'So where is he at the moment?' asked Ursula, whose beautiful face seemed marked by fatigue and anxiety.

'That's just the problem,' said Blake thoughtfully. 'It's not out of the question that he's still on the island. From now on, nobody should be on their own, particularly outside.'

'Better still, we should all leave, and as rapidly as possible,' exclaimed Ursula Brown.

'And go where?' asked Blake. 'There are only a couple of hours before dawn. Let's be patient,' he suggested in a soothing voice.

'Bill, it's awful,' moaned Madge, snuggled in her fiancé's arms after she'd led him down to her uncle's workshop at his request. 'We should never have come here. I've always been frightened of Uncle Gerry. I knew, I sensed it, I should have followed my instinct. And something tells me he hasn't left the island. I'm sure of it.'

'He must be very courageous if he's out there in the rain,' joked Bill, trying to calm his fiancée, who was on the brink of tears.

'I'm sure he's not far. I can feel his presence everywhere, in every room, even here. Are you quite sure it was he who played the part of Inspector Roy?'

'It's highly likely. But you're best placed to judge your uncle, Madge. Do you think his mind is twisted enough to have organised such a macabre evening?'

'I don't know. Sometimes I think so, sometimes not.'

'Well, I'm going to look around this workshop, because I've just had a thought about one little mystery.'

'A little mystery? Which one?'

'Give me time to check it, Madge. I'd look like a real idiot if I were wrong.' He examined the workbench and the shelving thoughtfully. 'By the way, did you ever find your handbag?'

'Yes, it was in my room after all. *But the letter was missing.*'

'Strange, very strange. If only you'd looked. Are you sure you brought it with you?'

'Absolutely sure. But what is it? You look as though you might have found something.'

Bill stared thoughtfully at the pillar drill.

'I believe so... But, come to think of it, there's still one thing I haven't told you—or anyone else, for that matter. At the time, I thought I'd dreamt it, but after what someone just told me... In fact, I wasn't very sure of myself when Dunbar brought up the incredible murder of Sergeant Hunt. Peter had seen the murderer, a sort of knight armed with a sword and wearing a long cloak. Blake had seen the same figure—but less distinctly—at the time of the first murder, climbing the tower. I was watching the tower at the same time, but from the south. I also thought I saw a figure climbing along the west wall. I could only make out a kind of long cloak flapping in the wind and moving slowly upward. But it was raining, there was a lot of wind and it was very dark. Add to that your uncle's constant allusions to the legends... I thought it was just my imagination playing tricks.'

Madge's eyes opened wide:

'So, you also think....'

'For now, I prefer to stick to the facts. I'd like you to be patient, also, while I check something out.'

Madge didn't even have time to protest as Bill disappeared through the door. As the seconds passed, her heart beat faster.

She was alone in the cellar.

She thought of her Uncle Gerry and his strange smile. Suddenly she heard footsteps in the corridor—footsteps which weren't Bill's. Approaching footsteps, which didn't appear to be in any hurry.

13

As he entered the tower room, Bill, out of breath from having climbed the interminable steps of the spiral staircase as fast as possible, ran into Gail Blake, who was just about to leave.

'Where are you going like that, my young friend?' asked the Cornish poet. 'Anyone would think the devil was hot on your heels.'

'No. Well, you see, Madge is all alone and I just wanted to check something quickly.'

Blake looked back at the room, perplexed:

'I'm afraid there's not much left to check. Everything's gone, except for Miss Brown's cloak—or, at least, what's left of it. The body, the murder weapon... all gone. Just like the Grail and the murderer.'

'The sword as well?'

'See for yourself.'

Bill stepped into the room, visibly disappointed.

'The same weapon was probably used to dispose of Hunt,' suggested Blake. 'You haven't seen his body yet, I assume? Come to think of it, we should bring it down to the castle. Otherwise, if it stays up there, the rain will wash all the clues away. What do you think?'

'We should ask Dr. Jerrold. But you're probably right. So, you think the murderer came back here to retrieve his weapon?'

'It seems logical. Dr. Jerrold could certainly tell us if we're right or not, once we get the body into a dry spot.'

'So how do you think the body disappeared from this room?'

Blake ran a nervous hand through his unruly hair.

'Even though the island is riddled with secret hiding places, I tend to think it's being tossed about by the waves, as we speak. Why did it have to disappear? That's easy: the killer didn't want it identified.'

'Unless a more thorough examination of the body would have revealed how he'd been able to commit the crime,' said Bill thoughtfully.

'Or both.'

'How and when did all this happen?'

'It was probably quite easy for him,' replied Blake, with a feline smile. 'We were down in the cellar, inspecting the workshop—in fact his own workshop! That confounded Pearson must have been laughing up his sleeve, pretending to be the inspector in charge of the enquiry. And, before that, in the library, speculating on the psychology *of his own personality!* Madge had just left, probably bored by the technical nature of our discussion, and then he left as well, ostensibly to see what had happened to Sergeant Hunt. In fact, he was going to see him for an altogether more sinister purpose. And there, I see two possibilities. The first is that Hunt was a minor player and Inspector Roy, alias Pearson, found some pretext to meet him on the upper promontory—where he was later found murdered—while he, Pearson, got rid of the body from this room.'

'Carrying him all by himself on that spiral staircase?'

'For a normal red-blooded male, it shouldn't have taken more than five minutes. Even a female could have done it, dragging the body by the heels.'

Bill had to agree.

'The other possibility has Sergeant Hunt in a more suspect role: helping his colleague dispose of the body, after which he was killed by a sword blow to the head. Given the scene of the second crime, it seems likely the first body was thrown into the sea from up there.'

'I definitely favour the first version,' said Bill, 'because there doesn't seem any point in lugging a body all the way up there, just to throw it in the sea. The small plateau with the sword in the stone would have done just as well.'

Blake, who appeared not to be listening, had gone over to the window. He grabbed the iron grill with both hand and shook it vigorously.

'So much for that,' he growled. 'It's firmly anchored. I came back to check. But it doesn't budge an inch. Not an inch.'

'Did you have a theory?'

'Yes and no. I thought it might have been possible to attach a rope—using a grappling hook, for example—and haul oneself up here. Difficult, but feasible. It's after that my theory fails to hold water. I thought there might be some sort of mechanism in the window, but I'm prepared to swear there isn't.'

Bill asked him about the shadow he thought he'd seen at the time of the crime.

'It's possible that I dreamt it all,' replied Blake gloomily, 'but Peter saw it as well. Speaking of Peter, where is he? The message he left in the hut struck me as very curious.'

A hesitant figure appeared in the doorway and, to her intense relief, Madge recognised Dr. Jerrold.

He came over:

'I was looking for you. They told me you were in the cellar. You look frightened. Is it because of me?'

Madge told him everything was all right. The man's voice and, in particular, his stare made her uneasy. He seemed to be able to read people's thoughts, but in an impersonal way; like an intelligent machine with a remarkable gift for observation.

'So, you were looking for me?' she asked.

'It's about your uncle.'

'We don't talk about him any more,' Madge replied curtly.

Dr. Jerrold stroked his chin thoughtfully.

'When I got his letter, I thought he was asking me, in a roundabout way, for a professional consultation. Then, after a few hours here, I began to think my role was to observe the human reactions to the situation in hand, and I continued to think that. But, after two murders, I've had to revise my opinion. Now, with hindsight, I believe I have a better understanding of the man, whom I observed less than his guests, even though he was the most visible person there.

'He spoke with considerable self-assurance. He knew exactly what he was doing, blowing hot and cold, slipping jokes and outrageous comments into his discourse one minute, and menacing remarks the next. He behaved like a host bent on keeping his audience on tenterhooks, during what he had promised would be an evening out of the ordinary. All of that was entirely to be expected, but... yes, there's a "but."'

Dr. Jerrold paused to take a cigarette out of its case and light it, without taking his eyes off Madge. He continued:

'Without wishing to appear pretentious, I must say that my profession has honed my powers of observation. And, when one speaks of observation, it's the reflective organ—to use the current expression—which is used more than the visual one. One has to look, of course, but one must above all be able to draw conclusions from one's observations. That's where the difficulty arises. Add to that experience, the other determining factor, and you will readily understand that it's only by combining these conditions that one may arrive at certain results, which, I flatter myself, I do rather well. What I'm saying, quite simply, is that I have considerable experience and I'm rarely mistaken.'

Madge had to bite her tongue not to remind him of her uncle's accusation that he, the great Dr. Jerrold, had committed a young woman to an asylum who wasn't by any measure insane.

'And I detected,' he continued, 'a strange look in his eye, particularly when he smiled.'

Madge became filled with dread. Granted Dr. Jerrold was a man full of his own importance, but she could not help but agree with him on this point.

'I believe I can assert, without fear of contradiction, that that strange look is not—to a degree which must, needless to say, be scientifically determined—that of a normal person.'

Madge was unable to utter a sound. She was now in utter fear of her uncle, all the more so because the suspicions she had harboured from an early age about her uncle had just been confirmed by an expert.

'There was another question I wanted to ask,' continued the psychiatrist, 'concerning your uncle's half-brother.'

'You think he might be the one murdered in the sealed room? And my uncle used him because of the strong resemblance?'

'It's an interesting hypothesis and quite plausible, for I believe his face was not burnt by accident. You didn't know him, if I recall correctly?'

'No. I repeat, I've never seen him.'

'Do you know what's become of him?'

'Nobody's talked about him for several years now. My father didn't consider him as one of his family. It's very simple: he never talked about him. I know that, when he was very young, he was placed in a special home. That's all I know.'

'What was he suffering from?' asked Dr. Jerrold, frowning.

'A mental illness, rather like the people you treat, that's all I know.'

'Some form of mental illness. Wait! Someone, I can't remember who, told me he liked the theatre and that once, he'd been invited to perform on stage. But that must go back quite a way.'

Dr. Jerrold's expression changed and Madge feared for a moment that he was in the grip of a seizure.

'I seem to recall,' he said after a few moments, 'that his name was Horatio?'

Madge nodded her agreement.

'That's what I was trying to remember. My God! We have to leave. We have to get everyone together.'

Ten minutes later, Dr. Jerrold spoke to all the assembled guests. The paleness of his complexion surprised them, and his brief declaration even more:

'Would everyone please gather their belongings. We have to leave the island immediately. I'll explain on the way. There's not a moment to lose!'

There was such determination in his voice that even the most headstrong among them obeyed without protest. His face betrayed a fear which was all the more palpable because it was constrained. A contagious fear which hastened the movements of all present.

A quarter of an hour later, luggage in hand, the little group left the castle. It was raining slightly less, but the wind had gained strength. They stopped in front of the watchman's shed. Peter still hadn't returned. They re-read his message and assumed that, after having witnessed the extraordinary second murder, the young watchman had decided to leave the island.

They quickly restarted their march, pausing not far from the footbridge, in a natural cutting through which the path ran. Madge and Ursula complained about the infernal pace set by the men, who seemed to have forgotten the good manners of yesteryear. But they were all waiting for Dr. Jerrold's explanation.

The setting was hardly propitious for what the doctor had to say. In almost total darkness, where they were only able to recognise each other by voice and by silhouette, their only surroundings were rocks lashed by a roaring and increasingly menacing sea, and drenched in a disagreeable fog of spray.

'I shan't feel safe until we're off this island,' announced Dr. Jerrold. 'But first, I want to go back over the insane events of this night and, in particular, over the psychological aspect of the crimes. We've all said, time and time again, that what we know doesn't make sense and doesn't follow any logic.

'*Well, that's just not true.* In fact, presided over by our host, we've been acting out an Arthurian drama, adopting the roles of Arthurian characters and living scenes with Arthurian artefacts like the Grail and the Sword in the Stone.'

'Still, there's one thing we haven't been able to recreate,' interjected Madge, 'and that's the Invisible Circle.'

'Luckily for us,' sighed Dr. Jerrold. 'So, seen in that light, there has been a certain logic and rhythm to the events. The murders themselves, even if they don't appear to have precise motives, still obey that same logic of the "Arthurian tragedy." You'll see what I mean in a moment.'

He gave a deep sigh and continued:

'Before I left to come here, I expressed to my wife my concern about the recklessness of some of my colleagues, all too ready to declare their patients cured. I said that after reading, to my utter stupefaction, of the release of "Horatio the Mad."'

Turning to Madge, he continued:

'That was the nickname the press gave at the time to the homicidal maniac, whom I have every reason to believe is the half-brother of your uncle, Miss Pearson. He was let out a month ago. I can readily understand why people have gone to great lengths not to talk to you about him. But, at this point, there can no longer be any doubt. You mentioned his name at the beginning of the evening, but I—alas!—failed to make the connection. It was only when you mentioned his love of the theatre....'

'My God,' murmured Madge, her hands covering her mouth.

'It is he, Horatio the Mad, with whom we have been dealing tonight. It was he who was our host; he who was Inspector Roy; he who was King Arthur, the dispenser of justice. I don't know what's happened to your Uncle Gerry, but we must fear the worst. This man is no ordinary criminal in the sense most people understand, because he is irresponsible. He's a madman, but an extremely lucid and intelligent one, which is why he's able to hide it. He looks like his half-brother Gerry, but is slightly older. Do I need to go on?

'He's passionate about plays and the theatre, and is very knowledgeable on the subject. He has a predilection for Greek tragedies and, thanks to his talent, after having given brilliant performances of them in the asylum, he was released some eight years ago. The doctors thought he was cured; I must stress that, at the time, he had not killed anyone. Oh, and I was forgetting: he cherished above all the legend of King Arthur and, shortly after his release, he produced a play featuring Guinevere, Lancelot, Morgan le Fay, Merlin the Enchanter and all the rest. It was entitled *The Return of King Arthur* and enjoyed an initial success in the small northern town where it ran. It happened at the fourth or fifth performance. It was he, Horatio, who was playing the role of King Arthur. Doesn't that ring a bell? It was about eight years ago.'

Jerrold paused for a moment before continuing:

'Right in the middle of the performance, before a packed audience, he unsheathed his sword and struck the actor opposite. At first, the audience thought, quite understandably, that the man on the floor, writhing in agony, was just acting. Horatio continued. I think he had killed or wounded half the cast before people realised they were watching a real massacre. I'll spare you the details. Horatio, encouraged by the play's initial success, had decided his role of the vengeful king needed more realism....'

It was almost pitch black and no one could see their neighbour's expression clearly, but the horror inspired by the psychiatrist's account was almost palpable. All the pieces of the puzzle had come together with a devastating logic.

Nobody needed to be asked twice when Jerrold suggested they start to move. This time, Madge and Ursula didn't lag behind and, a few minutes later, they could see the stone arch which spanned the water. The sight of it prompted a general sigh of relief. It seemed to signify the end of their nightmare.

Madge quickened her pace. She was ahead of the others when she stopped abruptly. Ursula, who was just behind her, heard her murmur "The Invisible Circle," and asked her what she was talking about. Bill, who had also overheard her, demanded:

'The invisible circle? What are you talking about?'

'It's an invisible circle,' stammered Madge, staring blindly at the stone arch. 'An imaginary circle, which can't be seen, but which is impossible to breach.'

They all followed her eyes and understood. Above the stormy sea, the natural arch, already partially collapsed, now presented an empty void in the middle. The wooden footbridge had disappeared.

'The invisible circle,' intoned Dr. Jerrold, in a lifeless voice. 'We're prisoners on this island... *And in the presence of a madman.*'

14

When Madge opened her eyes, she saw her room bathed in a celestial radiance. Through the window streamed a diffuse light, emanating from a golden halo. Was it morning? Was that even possible? Had the day put an end to the terrifying ordeal of the night?

For a few short moments she rubbed her eyes, savouring the moment of deliverance. Outside was a dense mist, which the morning sun tinted with a pink far less luminous than if it were a summer morning. But, after the grim darkness of the last few hours, even the pale dawn seemed dazzling.

She noticed another welcome element: the sea had calmed and one could hardly hear it or the wind, which had dropped. Even the occasional cries of the seagulls seemed less sinister than during the previous evening.

She had lived through a nightmare, she told herself, closing her eyes. She relived certain moments. When they had realised, after the collapse of the bridge, that they were well and truly prisoners on the island and at the mercy of a homicidal maniac, an unspeakable fear had seized them all. Ursula Brown had lost her self-control and only a solid slap from Gail Blake had calmed her down. Her journalist admirer had almost intervened, but had had to concede that Blake's action had been salutary, for, in that state, the slightest misstep would have consigned Ursula to a watery grave.

With the fear of death in their hearts, they had retraced their steps back to the castle with the inescapable feeling they were going back into the lion's mouth, rather than to a shelter. But what choice had they had? They had spent an hour in the lounge, warming themselves and discussing their fate. Any attempt to have crossed the arch, at least that night, would have ended in failure and only served to further the ends of the murderous madman. Their hopes, for the moment, rested on Peter Cobb's shoulders, for he would surely not have wasted a moment before alerting the authorities. Their most urgent priority was to protect each other while getting some sleep. They decided that the men would take turns standing guard over the guest rooms. Dunbar had been the first. Madge recalled hearing the journalist's footsteps as he paced up and down, before she fell into a deep slumber.

When she finally left her room, she was immediately reassured by the sympathetic smile of Josiah Hallahan, as he sat on a chair in the middle of the corridor.

She smiled back and, stifling a yawn, asked him what time it was.

'Nearly ten o'clock. But please don't make too much noise... she's still sleeping.'

He indicated Ursula's room and Madge remembered that Dr. Jerrold—who, fortunately, never went anywhere without his medicine bag—had administered a sedative before she had gone to her room.

'First, I must assure you that there was no further incident during the night. But you're not yet fully awake, it seems. Hurry up and go to the lounge, you'll find Blake has prepared a copious breakfast. And there's someone there who's anxious to see you. He hasn't been up very long.'

Madge found Bill seated in front of a steaming cup of tea and a mound of buttered toast.

Despite the concern on his weary face, he attempted a joke:

'A sumptuous décor and service of this quality, what more could one ask?'

As she sat down opposite him, Blake came over to ask whether she wanted tea or coffee. She opted for the tea and congratulated him on his talents as *maître d'hôtel.*

'I'm used to it,' replied the imposing poet. 'After all, I've been serving myself all these years. And whoever lives here has made sure the place is well-stocked. It's got everything we need.'

Madge suddenly looked around anxiously:

'But we're all alone! Where are the others? I don't see Dunbar or Jerrold.'

'They went down to take a look at the bridge to see what can be done—and also to see if they can attract anyone's attention.'

Madge's face expressed her disappointment:

'So nobody's come. I thought Peter would have alerted the police by now.'

'Patience, miss,' replied Blake reassuringly. 'It's only ten o'clock. I'm sure Jerrold and Dunbar won't be long. And with good news. As for Peter, he probably encountered the same difficulties we did, and was obliged to wait until morning. It'll take a bit of time for them to show up. No need to worry, for now.'

So saying, he left and returned with the teapot. Madge only began to feel awake after emptying half the cup, as Bill observed.

'Madge, my dear, the most important thing is to keep calm. If we start to panic, we'll be falling into that madman's hands.'

'Horatio. My God, I'd almost forgotten. He didn't show himself after....'

'No.'

'So possibly he's no longer on the island?'

Bill nodded pensively.

'Given the frenzy of events during the night and the sudden calm after we discovered the bridge had gone, it's tempting to think so. After putting on his macabre show with two dead bodies and all the other shock effects, he scarpered. At least, that's what probably happened. But it would be sheer foolishness on our part to declare victory and let down our guard. We have to remain vigilant and keep together as much as possible.'

'Of course,' replied Madge, placing her hand on his. 'But that's already good enough news. Last night, we were all convinced none of us would get out alive. Do you remember, after we marched back here in the rain—with Ursula practically out of her mind—we sat in front of the fire, expecting that maniac to emerge at any moment, brandishing his sword?'

'That's right, we were worried stiff. I'm not soon going to forget that night. But at last a lot of the mystery has been cleared up.'

'What do you mean?'

'I'm not talking about details, but the killer's general plan. At least some things are clear: we know we've been dealing with a madman obsessed with the Arthurian legends, with one idea in mind: to bring them to life, with himself in the role of the vengeful King Arthur. That's not a bad start, because before Dr. Jerrold's explanation, we were utterly in the dark. Who was our host? Who would be the victim? What game was he playing? Why the bodies? Et cetera.'

'But we still don't know the identity of the body in the tower, the one which disappeared. Was it Uncle Gerry?'

'There you have me. Particularly since he's now disappeared. In fact it could be anyone with a physical resemblance to our host. Uncle Gerry? Probable, alas! but not certain.'

'Well, if not, where is he?'

'Maybe absent for one reason or another. And Horatio took advantage of the situation to put on his macabre show. We'll have to wait and see.'

'And is the so-called Sergeant Hunt's body still up there on the cliff edge?'

'Yes, unless someone's made it disappear like the other one. No one's been back. We need to take care of it as soon as possible, but I'm afraid that, after all that rain, it won't yield any clues.'

Madge, who was buttering some toast, tried to put the dreadful image out of her mind.

'There are still quite a few mysteries left,' she sighed. 'The sword in the stone, the sealed room... it's all beyond me. But I remember you seemed to have an idea about that, last night?'

Madge's frown lent her adorable face an almost comic expression.

'Yes,' said Bill, smiling. 'And, given time, I'm sure I can crack that particular mystery.'

'Bill, tell me straight away. I hate secrets. Besides, there should never be any mysteries between us.'

'Please,' pleaded Bill. 'Just a couple of hours more, so I can verify certain theories. Then, I promise you, you'll be the first to know.'

Pretending to sulk, Madge drained her teacup. Suddenly her expression changed and Bill wondered if she had swallowed the hot tea too quickly.

'The "invisible circle", he announced that as well,' she whispered.

'Yes, we know.'

'Which means he did announce it. Do you remember what he said when someone asked him if the famous circle was already in effect? He said no, but it soon would be. So he knew very well what he was talking about. The collapse of the bridge wasn't caused by the sea, but by him. He sabotaged it to keep us on the island.'

'We already thought about that.'

'Thought about it? But it's absolutely certain, Bill! It's part of that madman's incredible stage production. And I refuse to believe that he would deprive himself of the spectacle of us cut off from the world and dying of fright.'

So, according to you, he must still be on the island. Let's not exaggerate the situation, Madge. Your reasoning is sound but, for my part, I feel optimistic,' said Bill, whose expression belied his words.

15

The psychiatrist and the journalist were back before noon. Without appearing too pessimistic, they were not wearing the happy smiles that portend good news. The mist had been too thick to see anyone on the promenade at the other side of the bridge.

Ursula had not left her bed all morning and she stayed there through lunch, joined by her gallant knight Dunbar. As for the others, they did not eat much: their topic of conversation—the past antics of Horatio—hardly being one to whet the appetite. Everyone remembered the case which had dominated the headlines at one time. As for Madge, it had never occurred to her that the perpetrator could be her uncle by marriage: the crime was too horrible. And she was thankful to the members of her entourage for keeping it from her, for she was sure that having such a murderer in the family would have haunted her for a long time. After she had pointed out firmly that there was no direct link between her and that horrible individual, Bill suggested they change the subject and discuss the afternoon's assignments. Madge and Hallahan were chosen to watch the bridge, while the others would conduct a comprehensive inspection of the island.

Around two o'clock, Hallahan, armed with an old pair of binoculars which he had found in the cellar, was scanning the coastline across the bridge.

'Still nothing?' asked Madge, sitting on a rock, her elbows on her knees and her fists under her chin.

'Nothing,' replied the history professor. 'But that's not surprising with this heavy mist. You can see the path that goes from the other side of the bridge, but higher up is something else. And I wonder if it would be wise for anyone to walk along those cliffs in this weather.'

Madge looked around and, once again, had the impression of living a dream. The shroud of pearl-coloured mist which enveloped them gave the island an almost phantasmagorical appearance under the pale, diffuse outline of the sun. A mild, sluggish day which contrasted strikingly with the turbulence of the night before. Apart from the steady backwash of the waves and the slight breeze, all was calm, strangely so for this place.

'If you look for too long,' continued Hallahan, 'you start to imagine things.'

'Uncle Gerry once told me the place was populated by ghosts.'

'It's true, this part of the world is rich in legends. But my eyes are getting tired.'

Hallahan lowered his binoculars and came over to sit by Madge.

'It's a strange region, isn't it,' he asked after a while.

'Yes, fascinating even. But I don't think I'm entirely objective. I have memories of my childhood which have marked me for life, but not alas! in the good sense. It was always a great relief to get back home after each agonising holiday.'

'How old were you?'

'Nearly ten. I was alone with Uncle Gerry. I think it amused him to torment me and frighten me.'

'I think he was quite a practical joker.'

'Maybe, but in any case he scared me.'

'You seem to have a very bad impression of him, miss. Why did you accept his invitation, then?'

Madge sighed:

'If only I knew.'

Hallahan stroked his white beard thoughtfully, then observed:

'In fact, I hardly knew him, as I've said before. But I believe folks have formed an excessively unfavourable impression of him.'

'They say you only see the good side of people.'

'Possibly. But so far, it seems to work pretty well.'

'And what do you think of Horatio?'

'That's different. The man is obviously sick.'

'Maybe, but there's no good in him.'

'How do you know? You say you've never met him.'

'Luckily, because… But we have! Didn't we see him in yesterday's production, playing the role of my uncle and then that of a police inspector? Not to mention those two remarkable murders. Great art, you have to admit. We hung on his every word for several hours on end while he led us by the nose, taking us through the meanderings of his mad, Machiavellian plan.'

'I don't think anger is of very much use in this affair. The better we get to know him, the better we can confront him.'

Madge sat up straight:

'So, you think he's on the island as well?'

'I don't know, I'm just assuming the worst.'

There was a silence.

'What good can there possibly be in him?' exclaimed Madge, exasperated by Hallahan's impassivity.

'According to Dr. Jerrold, he's highly intelligent.'

'Diabolically so!'

'He also has a passion for the Arthurian legends.'

'And look where that led him. A passion which has already resulted in the deaths of several people.'

'You're not from around here, are you?' asked Hallahan calmly. 'Neither am I, actually, but I admit I'm in love with the place: the earth, its roots and its legends.'

'In love with Vivian also, Mr. Merlin the Enchanter?'

Madge, who was watching him out of the corner of her eye, could not suppress the amusement this strange and anachronistic history professor provoked in her, with his long, white beard and his old-fashioned clothes. The look in his blue eyes was both mischievous and wise.

'Have I ever denied it?' he asked, perfectly serious. 'This old bachelor is *still seeking* Vivian. I've never seen her, even though I've known about her since I was a young lad, and I feel her always by my side.'

For a few moments, Madge wondered if he was about to flirt with her, and began to think this old man in his sixties lacked neither charm nor class. Her pride was a little hurt when she realised he could only think of the imaginary Vivian, who had seduced him at a tender age, when he had heard, read and re-read the legends which would dominate his life, determine his profession and occupy most of his spare time.

"To hear him describe this imaginary Vivian," thought Madge, "this man would drive mad with jealousy any woman who had the misfortune to marry him." His interest in the legends appeared not to have diminished one iota from the day he discovered the fabulous exploits of the Knights of the Round Table.

He was a remarkable storyteller, with a soft, calm, evocative voice. Time rushed by as she listened, transported, as he described in great detail many of the little-known aspects of the legends. She felt she could really hear the chimes of bells in the far distance as he described the tragic end of Lyonesse, a nearby island, which sank one night into a furious ocean. Sometimes, behind the sound of the waves, the fishermen of the region still hear the ringing of the bells of the one hundred and forty churches engulfed in the tragedy.

It was past four o'clock when he stopped, and no one had appeared on the cliffs opposite.

'Still nobody,' observed Madge. 'I'm starting to worry about Peter. He's had quite enough time to bring the police. We can't spend another night here.'

Hallahan looked at the broken arch below:

'With a long enough rope and a grappling hook, it should be possible to cross the bridge... if there were something to attach to on the other side.'

'Dr. Jerrold said it was impossible.'

Hallahan picked up the binoculars again.

'He's probably right. If we found a rope, and especially a grappling hook, we could always try. But it would be very perilous for the one who had to perform the acrobatics. It would only need for the hook to be badly anchored on the other side and he would break every bone in his body.'

'When the tide's out, I heard it's possible to cross by jumping from one rock to another.'

'Even though it's out at this very moment, it's far from being what I would call a smooth sea. No, really, that way seems just as dangerous as the other. The rocks are devilishly slippery and the area is strewn with reefs. Even an experienced swimmer could not avoid them at the slightest movement of the waves. Obviously, it's not entirely impossible, but can we really afford to lose one of our members in an attempt to reach the other side?'

Madge shuddered, thinking of Bill who, because of his age, would inevitably be the one chosen.

'No, of course not. By the way, I checked the bridge when we got here. At the spot where it broke away, it seems to have been natural.'

'On this side, yes, but not the other. You can see it through the binoculars. There are splinters in the two places where it broke, meaning that the wood was cut.'

Madge took the binoculars and verified that what her companion had claimed was correct.

'But,' she observed, 'if the bridge was sabotaged on the other side, doesn't that mean that Horatio has gone? That he's not on the island any more? He must have cut the bridge *after* he'd crossed it.'

'Not necessarily. Haven't you noticed the part of the bridge which has been ripped away? It's down there to the south, floating between two reefs.'

After a moment, Madge succeeded in locating it.

'Yes, I see it, but it's quite far away. There's a rope attached. Yes, I see it.'

Hallahan dropped his voice.

'You can do a lot of things with a rope. For example, wrap it around a boulder and jam a chock under the boulder made of something that dissolves in water, such as certain salt crystals. When the sea rises to a certain level, the salt dissolves and the boulder, which is in unstable equilibriums, rolls and takes with it the bridge, suitably sawn beforehand. There are other methods, but that's enough to show how the bridge could have been sabotaged to rupture at a predetermined hour, which means that the author of that little trick *didn't necessarily leave the island.*'

16

'Hello there,' said Blake's penetrating voice as he came slowly down the path. 'Don't you have pins and needles? Still no one? I'm taking over, Hallahan, you can go back to the castle. Mr. Professor planned to keep this sweet young thing all to himself all afternoon? It's my turn now.'

The imposing Cornishman sat down next to them.

'You seem to be full of beans,' observed Josiah Hallahan. 'Does that mean there's some good news?'

'Neither good nor bad. We've finished exploring the island and it seems there's no one here but us.'

After Hallahan had left—mischievously warning Madge about lifelong bachelors—she asked after Bill.

'He's doing just fine,' replied Blake. 'Don't worry about him. At this very moment, he's in the process of sniffing every stone in the tower, like a hunting dog. He's got an idea at the back of his mind, that's for sure.'

'Yes, he told me about it,' agreed Madge.

'Just before I left, he showed me something at the top of the wall. He seems to be on to something. Of course, a lot of details are clearer in the light of day.'

'And, needless to say, he didn't tell you any more than that.'

'He's very secretive.'

'And the "something," what was it?'

'A hook. A solid hook. In the rafter supporting the roof. It sticks out a bit, just above the window.'

'A hook, as in something you can attach a rope to? So the murderer did get up there.'

Blake shrugged his shoulders.

'That explains the figure we saw at the time of the crime, on a section of the wall, that's all. I still don't see how a person of flesh and bone could have passed through the protective grill. Anyway, we shall see what we shall see.'

Madge appeared worried for a moment, then she passed the binoculars to her companion, indicating the detached part of the bridge and explaining what she thought had happened.

'It's not impossible for someone to have escaped our search by hiding in a crevice in the ground,' he conceded, 'but if Horatio is still on the island, he's more likely to have hidden in the castle itself. But we have a plan for tonight. By the way, we recovered the body of the so-called sergeant and put it in the cellar. Dr. Jerrold certifies he was killed by a sword, and very probably the one which disappeared. Terrible wounds, inflicted with great violence, as if he'd been hounded—.'

'If you go on like that, you can keep watch by yourself,' threatened Madge, making as if to get up. 'Although he's not a pet, Professor Hallahan talked to me about fairies, wizards and princes....'

Gail Blake couldn't help smiling in amusement behind his thick beard.

'Why hide the truth? We're alone on this island, cut off from the outside world, imprisoned inside an "invisible circle," and probably with a homicidal maniac for company.'

'I'm going back.'

'Alone? Hallahan's already quite a long way ahead.'

'Then stop.'

'If you wish. But it doesn't change the facts.'

With a boldness which surprised even herself, Madge stared at her companion. What kind of man was hiding inside that massive build; behind the savage and mocking face; under that wild shock of black hair?

'You're a poet, aren't you?' she asked point blank.

'A little bit, yes. Even though I mostly write stories for certain magazines and tales for children. Does that surprise you?'

'I imagined poets differently.'

'How?'

'I don't know. Perhaps more dreamy.'

Blake smiled and looked heavenwards.

'I often watch the clouds go by... I can tell you, for example, that the bad weather is coming back tonight.'

'You're trying to frighten me again.'

'I'm a Cornishman, miss.'

'I didn't know that scaring people was a local speciality. But if you say so....'

'Look around you. Look at the landscape: harsh, wild and forbidding. Why would the people who live here be any different?'

When Madge didn't answer, he gave a thunderous peal of laughter. 'Which doesn't mean we're heartless and don't know how to amuse ourselves. Come to one of our festivals and you'll see.

'But look at the jagged coastline, the craggy rocks and that wild sea. They translate into a proud, independent and inflexible character.

'Now imagine the night of a storm, one much more violent than last night's. Listen to the roar of the ocean; look at the waves arching their monstrous backs; imagine liquid mountains which melt; hear the storm growl, its *yataghans* of fire cleaving the racing clouds. Can you hear the howls of the tempest, like hungry wolves?'

'The children who read your stories mustn't sleep a wink at night.'

'I'm afraid you still don't understand our sense of humour. But, believe me, you will soon, my dear little lady.'

Madge was slow to respond:

'There's one person here who seems to have a particularly peculiar sense of humour.'

'You're talking about Horatio?'

Madge nodded.

'Well, yes,' replied Blake thoughtfully. 'It could be considered an extreme form of humour.'

'More like paranoiac delirium. He's a dangerous madman!'

'No doubt about it. No one would disagree.'

'But when you talk about him, you don't seem at all fearful.'

The poet's black eyes took on a determined and vindictive look.

'Well, no, actually. I'm waiting for him to show himself. Then he'll find out what an old Cornishman like myself is capable of doing to him.'

The clock was striking half past six by the time Blake and Madge reached the castle. The sun was going down, and their chances of contacting anyone on the mainland with it. Everyone was assembled in the lounge except Ursula, still locked in her room. The plan was for Madge to keep her company, while the men inspected the castle from top to bottom, sealing each space after it was searched, so that the whole place virtually became a fortress during the night. Hammers, nails and planks were all ready.

Madge found Ursula lying on her bed, still looking very pale. The fading light created shadows in every corner of the room and accentuated the young woman's sick appearance.

'Have you caught cold?' asked Madge, taking a seat near the bed.

'No, there's no fever....'

She spoke the words in a quavering voice and her hands were trembling slightly.

'... and no sore throat. I think....'

'Yes?'

'The idea that this madman might still be on the island is driving me insane, too. I get dizzy, so I prefer to stay lying down. In any case, Dr. Jerrold has given me some medicine and forbidden me to leave the room.'

For the first time, Madge felt sympathy for Ursula. Seeing her like that, weak and defenceless, and having lost her superb looks, Madge felt nothing but pity.

'I'm very highly strung, in fact,' Ursula continued. 'And when it starts, I don't know what I'm doing any more. I lose all self-control and am ready to do almost anything, such as throwing myself in the water, for example.'

'And have you always been like that?'

Ursula looked strangely at Madge:

'No, not always. Only since I met... a certain person.'

'My uncle?'

Ursula nodded solemnly.

'After three months here, I was never the same again. My nerves were completely shattered. I know that when you listen to him—or whoever passed himself off as him—I'm as malicious as the wicked fairy of the legend. I know I haven't always behaved perfectly towards my companions, but your uncle....'

Madge told her about the childhood vacations passed in his company.

'So, you must understand,' said Ursula. 'But please realise that what I endured was of a whole other dimension. Less frightening, perhaps, but more cruel.'

'Cruel? I'm afraid I don't understand. Did he mistreat you?'

'No, it's not what you think. It's difficult to explain. Let me give you an example. When he suggested I come and stay here, he held out the prospect of the life of a queen. I admit being disappointed at first. Then, after having said that I was what the place needed to restore its prestige, he told me that, on second thoughts, he hadn't really made a decision about the future. And so on. He drove me crazy.'

There was a peculiar gleam in Ursula's blue-green eyes as she recalled her past disappointment. Madge was starting to get a clearer idea of their relationship. There was no doubt the woman was a gold-digger who had met her match in Uncle Gerry. A thwarted and bitter gold-digger who clearly had not yet found what she was seeking. As for Uncle Gerry, doubtless dazzled by Ursula's remarkable beauty, he must have derived great pleasure from toying with his delectable prey.

'Luckily, I found the strength to leave. Besides, what did I lose?' She looked disdainfully about her. 'This place can't be worth much.'

'Not a great fortune, I would have to say,' replied Madge.

'Nothing. The land doesn't belong to him. He only owns this ruin. But you must know all that, being his sole heiress, in all likelihood.'

'I've never thought about it.'

Ursula shrugged.

'You're talking about him as if his death was a fact, but we know no such thing.'

'What difference does it make?' retorted Ursula brusquely. 'You don't love him any more than I do, do you?'

Madge didn't know how to reply.

'Now we know where his perverse nature comes from,' said Gerry Pearson's ex-fiancée. 'He had a lot on his plate with that crazy half-brother. It's their mother who wasn't quite right in the head, I believe. What was she called?'

'Ruth,' said Madge pensively. 'I never saw her either. For all I know, there was nothing abnormal about her.'

'She was very beautiful, they say.'

'That's what I heard. She suffered from severe nervous depression. Sometimes she even forgot who she was. She sometimes disappeared for days at a time in the forest. But it seems that form of depression is more common than we think.'

'Look who you're talking to. Besides, if this goes on, I shall go mad myself. This interminable wait… and still nothing. I wonder what the young watchman is doing.'

'We were just talking about it. Bill thinks the unfortunate fellow has been murdered as well. He did leave a note before he left, but that proves nothing. Anybody could have written it. Even if he did, Horatio could have caught him before he managed to leave the island, and thrown his body in the water. That's what everyone thinks. Otherwise, he'd have had plenty of time to alert the police, and we wouldn't still be here.'

'It's terrifying,' murmured Ursula, reaching out for the glass of water on the bedside table. 'Terrifying.'

Ursula repeated the word several times, like a litany, staring blindly at the opposite wall.

'In fact, I've never been at ease here,' she continued, 'and I've always felt a sort of unrest. But now I sense a real presence. I sense the danger is very near, as faithful as a shadow, but I can't locate it.'

A shiver ran up Madge's spine. It was exactly how she was feeling. A close, almost palpable, danger but as elusive and invisible as a breath of air.

17

By eight o'clock, all the doors and windows of the "fortress" had been nailed shut. After a meticulous search, the occupants were certain that Horatio could not be inside the walls. They dined, therefore, in an atmosphere of relative security, chatting about this and that until coffee was served. Ursula had come out of her room to join them. The terrifying thought of Horatio only returned when Blake proposed summarising where things stood.

'The madman may not have left the island,' he declared, 'but we're sure he's not inside the castle. Remember that the building only has three doors leading to the outside: the entrance, the postern gate which leads to the plateau with the sword in the stone, and the one opening onto the path leading to the summit of the island. Each of them is locked and bolted, solidly bolted. Absolutely impossible to get in without smashing them open. The same for the windows, every shutter is closed.

'On the ground floor, only the room we're in now has no shutters, but it has glass panels embedded in lead and it's impossible to break a window without alerting everybody. Similarly, we've locked the cellar and nailed all the openings shut. To get into this place now, you would need an axe or a battering ram.'

'You're talking about a normal person,' interjected Dr. Jerrold from behind the gently curling smoke of his cigarette. 'Horatio the Mad *isn't a normal person*. Haven't you understood yet?'

'Explain yourself.'

'To start with, he seems to have no difficulty passing through walls. He's proved that by murdering someone in a locked and sealed room.'

'It was hocus-pocus, pure and simple.'

'Pure and simple? That's rich. Explain it, then.'

'I admit I don't know, but this young man has an idea, unless I'm mistaken,' replied Blake, turning to Bill.

'I think I'm on to something, yes,' confirmed Bill, slightly embarrassed.

'Explain yourself,' ordered Dr. Jerrold curtly.

'It's simple. I believe I've discovered how Horatio committed the first murder.'

The doctor's smile was sceptical and mocking.

'Including how he removed the sword from the stone?'

'Of course, because that riddle is directly linked to the quasi-magical method of committing the crime. Or, if you prefer, once the first riddle is solved, the rest is obvious, or almost. But I don't think that's the most important thing at the moment. What we have to do, before anything else, is make sure we're safe, here, tonight, and think about how we're going to leave the island tomorrow. Because it's out of the question we stay another night.'

'That's understood. But we'd like to satisfy our curiosity, none the less. The crime is too extraordinary for us to leave it there, Mr. Page. You've said too much... or not enough. We're listening.'

Bill drained his cup calmly, before an audience hanging on his every word.

'Right,' he said. 'But I warn you, I haven't any proof. The ideal would be to recover the sword.'

'To do that, you'd have to take it out of the hands of the murderer,' sneered Blake.

'I leave that up to you.'

'You'll see. If he turns up tonight, I swear I'll recover the sword.'

'Let's hope he doesn't turn up,' said Bill prudently. 'To get back to the first crime, let me remind you all that you, Mr. Blake, and I vaguely saw a figure climbing up the side of the tower. Was it an illusion, a phantasmagoria due to nervous strain? That's what each of us believed until we compared notes on our testimony. It seemed highly unlikely that the murderer could have scaled the wall with all that wind and rain. He would have needed a rope. That thought came back to me this afternoon when I noticed a solid hook screwed into one of the rafters supporting the roof above the window. I knew then that I was on the right track.

'Was there a rope already in place when the fake Gerry Pearson, alias Horatio, invited us to inspect the room? Probably. No one looked outside, and in any case the iron grill would have prevented it. Someone would have had to put their hand through in order to touch the rope, which could have been kept out of sight by a nail in the window jamb. The rope would have been looped around the hook, so that when the operation was over and the murderer was back on the ground, he could pull on one end to bring the whole rope down. The rope needed to be knotted to facilitate the climb, and there was probably a ring level with the window, to steady him once he got there.'

'All right, so he used a rope to climb up,' replied Jerrold impatiently. 'It's what he did afterwards that interests us.'

'I'll tell you,' replied Bill, with a wicked gleam in his eye, 'but only part of it.'

'What do you mean, "only part of it"?' asked the psychiatrist irritably.

'I need to talk to someone first, for personal reasons, that's all. Rest assured, Doctor, I shan't keep you waiting long.'

Madge, who had been watching Bill closely, realised that he was referring to the promise he'd made to her earlier that she would be the first to know. As for Dr. Jerrold, seeing him pester her fiancé, she found herself enjoying his annoyance and displeasure. He was not used to anyone else being master of the situation.

'Fine, fine,' he said through gritted teeth. 'Go on.'

'So, shortly after we leave the room, the murderer arrives at the base of the tower, climbs up the rope to be level with the window, and hangs there by clipping his belt to the ring, much as alpinists do. Then he beckons to his accomplice inside the room. The accomplice who will become his victim.'

'Now I'm not following you at all,' interjected Jerrold once again. 'The man we left in the sealed room, whom we took to be Gerry Pearson, was Horatio himself, was he not? And now you're telling us it was he who climbed up the rope. Which is it? He can't be both at once.'

'There was certainly a substitution at one point.'

'When we were up in the room?'

'Yes. Probably when we were busy searching the place—at his suggestion, by the way. We were very preoccupied and the light was poor, do you remember: the little oil lamp and those storm lamps. Suppose the accomplice had followed us up the spiral staircase and waited next to the door. At the right moment, Horatio slips out of the door and his accomplice takes his place.'

'But we saw him after the search. He spoke to us and gave us what we needed to seal the room. It was the same person.'

'His voice? I seem to remember he was constantly clearing his throat and he spent quite a bit of time lighting a fire. And you're forgetting one thing, Jerrold: we were dealing with actors. I've no proof, of course, but I'm pretty sure that the accomplice was one of the loonies he met in the asylum, with a gift for the theatre like himself. Neither is playing the part of the other, but both of them are playing Gerry Pearson, of whom none of you has a clear souvenir. They naturally use what they have in common to create this fake personage. And, by the way, didn't we find a room with a dressing table and tons of make-up? I'm surprised you appear to have forgotten that, Dr. Jerrold. We're victims of a stage production, a crazy play put on by a mad actor with a pathologically devious mind.'

'It's true,' murmured Jerrold, shaken to the core. 'A pathologically devious mind. That's it exactly.'

'This man has toyed with us. We've been docile marionettes and he the serene manipulator, the brilliant master of the situation, reviving for his own sick pleasure a medieval tragedy. And what about his role as Inspector Roy? What mastery! I fell for it like a ton of bricks when he sent me to the village to knock on the door of a police station that wasn't there.'

'What's even more amazing,' said Hallahan, 'is that he actually put us on the right track. He drew our attention to the Arthurian legends when we found ourselves in the library.'

'And, from what I've been told, he even drew your attention to the shavings next to the drill. Which represent, as I shall explain at the right time, a vital clue. So, while playing his role, he was nevertheless guiding our investigation in the right direction. What a nerve, and what satisfaction for his deranged mind to manipulate us so easily. And let's not forget the cloak drenched in meths. It was he who detected traces of the fuel. And it was true, of course, *because that's exactly what he'd done*. At the right moment, Miss Brown, he'd taken your cloak and soaked it in methylated spirits.

'Let me get back to the explanation. He's up by the window. His accomplice, who trusts him and obeys his every order, doesn't think twice when he calls him to the window and asks him to turn round. He drives the sword between the poor fellow's shoulders and holds him there like a chicken on a spit. Meanwhile, he brings the piece of material soaked in alcohol out of his pocket, wraps it round the other's face and sets fire to it. He had to do that, otherwise, looking closely, we might discover the victim's face had been made up. After that, he pushed the body towards the centre of the room.'

'But it's not possible,' exclaimed Dunbar. 'The sword couldn't get through the grill.'

'And it hadn't been doctored,' added Blake. 'I examined it myself.'

'I know,' said Bill, looking sorrowful. 'But you're forgetting it's a magic sword. And don't forget the presence of the Grail in the room, which also fosters miracles. The Grail, which then disappeared... But I've already said too much. With all those elements, you're bound to stumble on the explanation of the puzzle which—.'

Bill stopped suddenly.

A loud noise had interrupted him.

18

'The wind's getting up,' said Dr. Jerrold, who had jumped like everyone else at the sudden noise.

'The wind doesn't make that kind of noise,' said Blake.

'Maybe something fell down?'

'It didn't sound like a vase falling.'

Other theories were advanced, all equally confusing:

'It was outside.'

'It was in the courtyard, I think.'

'No, upstairs.'

'I think it came from the cellar.'

'From the cellar!' exclaimed Ursula. 'My God, that's where they took the body.'

'Wait, let's all calm down.'

The noise occurred a second time, freezing all present for a few seconds.

'It's a shutter banging,' said Dr. Jerrold. 'Just as I said, it's the wind.'

'I think you may be right,' said Gail Blake, 'but we need to check. Stay here, I'll take a tour outside.'

'No, it's too dangerous,' said Hallahan. 'It's pitch black. If it's one of the murderer's tricks, he'll have you before you know it.'

'I'm ready and waiting.'

'Better to check from the inside. Let's form three groups and each take a floor.'

Josiah Hallahan's suggestion was adopted. Bill went to the second floor with Madge. Dr. Jerrold, Dunbar and Ursula took the first floor. Blake and Hallahan stayed on the ground floor.

Ten minutes later, the journalist and Ursula announced they'd found the offending shutter and it wouldn't bang anymore. It was past nine. All the activity had exhausted Ursula, who went back to her room after having pleaded with Dr. Jerrold to give her a powerful sleeping draught; even though extremely tired, she feared she would be unable to fall asleep otherwise. Dunbar, armed with a packet of cigarettes and a bottle of whisky, decided to install himself on a chair and keep watch on the corridor "without taking my eyes off her door for a second," as he declared defiantly.

The others went back to the lounge. But shortly afterwards there was more banging. On the assumption that it was another loose shutter they went off on another search of the premises, but this time it was less organised. Apart from Bill and Madge, who stayed together, the others inspected the floors alone. In the middle of the investigation, yet another noise shook the castle. Bill and Madge, on the ground floor, rapidly discovered the cause: the door opening onto the little courtyard had been flung back against the wall by the wind. The psychiatrist, the poet and the history professor hurried to join them.

'It's blowing like the devil,' said Hallahan, looking at the sky. 'I think there's going to be a heavy storm.'

The wind whistled in the rooftops of the castle, carrying along thick black clouds which obscured the light of the moon as they passed.

'All right,' said Dr. Jerrold nervously, 'maybe it was the wind which caused the door to bang. But it didn't open by itself.'

'But we didn't nail that one shut,' replied Blake. 'It opens onto the courtyard, not the outside.'

'I'm not talking about nails. I'm talking about the handle. I say it couldn't have been the wind, no matter how violently it was blowing.'

'Somebody must not have shut it properly.'

'Please, gentlemen, let's not lose our self-control. I really can't believe it was Horatio. How could he be all over the place opening that door and those shutters? First of all, how could he have got in here, in—.'

The professor didn't finish. A terrible scream interrupted him, echoing lugubriously around the castle. Madge pressed against Bill, screaming in turn.

'My God,' murmured Hallahan, 'it sounds as though someone's just had their throat cut.'

'It came from the cellar,' said Blake. 'I'm going to take a look.'

Hallahan tried to stop him, but in vain. His friend was already at the end of the corridor. From then on, confusion and panic reigned.

Jerrold took off on his own. Doors could be heard banging and there were footsteps on the stairs. Each followed his own idea. At one point, there was the sound of breaking glass, but, in the general confusion, not everybody heard it. Then, a little later, the voice of Dr. Jerrold could be heard over the tumult, calling everyone to Ursula's room. Madge ran up the old staircase and reached the room out of breath. She saw Dunbar, Bill and Dr. Jerrold by the bed, forming a circle around a deathly pale Ursula, who was huddled back against the headboard of the bed. The journalist said it was she, terrified by all the noises, who had screamed.

'He's here. He—he's come back to the castle,' she stammered, shivering in her nightgown. 'I can feel it. He's very close. He made all those noises.'

With infinite patience, Dr. Jerrold explained it was only a couple of badly fitting shutters which the wind had caused to bang. But he couldn't shake the visibly terrified young woman's conviction. He left the room, returned with his medicine bag, and asked all present to leave her alone. Closing the door behind her, Madge couldn't suppress a shiver on seeing the metallic reflection of the syringe the psychiatrist had just pulled out of his bag.

As she was about to go back downstairs, she heard an urgent voice behind her:

'Miss, could I speak to you for a second?'

Madge turned to face Frank Dunbar. The journalist had already seemed ill at ease the night before, when they'd been introduced, but now his appearance was downright bilious. Fear? Perhaps. Whisky? Certainly. His eyes and breath testified to it. But under the surface Madge detected a tormented soul.

'I'm listening.'

'I'm very worried.'

'Aren't we all?'

'Oh, it's not my own safety I'm worried about, believe it or not. Horatio would be doing me a service by decapitating me.'

'*Decapitating you?*' repeated Madge, startled, her eyes wide. 'Why are you thinking about such a horrible death?'

'I said it instinctively. It's the kind of death you tend to think about when there's a homicidal maniac with a sword wandering about the place.' Madge seemed visibly to fall apart. 'But that's not what I'm talking about. It's Ursula I'm worried about. She's already highly-strung by nature and I'm afraid this madhouse and this atmosphere, not to mention all that's happened will cause her to lose her head. Sorry, I meant lose her mind.

'Ursula's case is different, you must agree. I was posted in front of her door when she screamed. I had a shock, I don't mind telling you. At the time, I thought someone had slit her throat.'

'I can understand. But how can I be of help?'

Dunbar lowered his eyes.

'Ursula and I are... old friends. Old friends who haven't seen each other for a long time, and I'm still very fond of her.'

'I'd already worked that out.'

'We met just after she'd been involved with your uncle. That's why....'

'Uncle Gerry never spoke about her, I can promise you that. And, besides, I didn't know she existed until yesterday.'

'That's not what I'm getting at. It's about your uncle. You knew him pretty well, didn't you?'

Madge looked hard at the reporter.

'I don't know where you're going with all this.'

'I've every reason to believe that he's the one who made Ursula like this, who made her a nervous wreck.'

Madge had already been taken into the young woman's confidence and, although she shared her sentiments, she was beginning to tire of the endless attacks on her family members.

'I repeat, I knew nothing about their affair.'

The reporter didn't appear to have heard.

'At one point, I thought she was making up the stuff about their relationship, but now I don't think she exaggerated one little bit. Behind that façade of the sophisticated landed gentry, Gerry Pearson is a disgusting, depraved individual with—.'

'Let me remind you it's not him we're dealing with, but his half-brother Horatio, altogether more dangerous. Besides, it's more than likely that he killed Uncle Gerry in the meantime.'

The journalist sighed:

'I think, if I knew more about what happened between them back then, I could help Ursula more.'

'The best thing would be to ask *her*.'

Dunbar moved close enough to touch Madge and a disquieting look came into his eye:

'He's the one I want to talk to. Him, your Uncle Gerry.'

'I just told you he's probably dead, murdered by that madman.'

'Tell me what you know about him, miss. It's very important.'

He was clutching her arm now and Madge was very relieved to hear Bill's voice from the bottom of the stairs, asking them to come to the lounge immediately.

She took the stairs two at a time and hurtled into the room. Then she stopped dead. Before she could notice the worried faces of Bill and Hallahan, she had already taken in the gravity of the situation. She at once realised the significance of the noise of breaking glass she had heard earlier: the lattice window had been broken.

The fresh, moist air of the night was filling the room and affecting the flame flickering in the hearth. But the wind, despite its force, could not have caused the damage. Only a violent blow of human origin could have created such a breach in the fortress. Now there was no longer any doubt: *the fox was in the henhouse.*

19

Dunbar arrived, followed by Dr. Jerrold. The former looked puzzled and the latter changed his expression. Many minutes went by before a word crossed either pair of lips.

'It must have happened a few minutes before I got back here,' observed Hallahan. 'I heard a noise as I was coming up from the cellar. *He* could be anywhere in the castle by now.'

Bill went over to the broken window and examined it:

'After all, it didn't require any great effort to do. A good shove in the right place... let's look outside.'

'Bill! Be careful,' cried Madge as he leaned out of the window.

'It's about six feet to the ground from here,' he said, 'but there's a buttress just under the window you can climb on easily. He could have stood there and broken the window without any problem. God only knows where he is now.'

A deathly silence followed his words. Madge, who had just turned away, was suddenly gripped by terror. An image swam before her eyes: a man sitting on the throne wearing a gold crown and a flamboyant cape, smiling amiably at her. Serene, calm and confident. King Arthur?

In his right hand he held the famous Holy Grail, in his left a sword. A symbolic image which seemed to have a particular significance, but which Madge was unable to determine.

The tip of the sword was dark, as if it had been dipped in the thick liquid which flowed slowly down the blade... A liquid the colour of blood.

Madge shuddered and blinked her eyes in an attempt to erase the image, to no avail. She approached "King Arthur" in order to get a closer look at his face. He resembled Uncle Gerry, but a terrifying Uncle Gerry with a horrible smile and an unbearable gaze gleaming with madness... *Horatio the Mad*.

'The situation is desperate,' said Hallahan solemnly as he went over to Bill, who was on his knees examining the shards of broken glass.

'Too desperate for us to waste time looking for clues here. It's obvious that Horatio has managed get into the castle and could be anywhere right now.'

'My God,' shouted Dunbar. '*Ursula... she's all alone.*'

He left the room and they could hear his frantic footsteps on the stairs.

Hallahan had vainly made a gesture calling for calm. Suddenly a worried expression crossed his face. His gaze swept the room and stopped at Dr. Jerrold.

'Where's Blake? Has anyone seen him?'

'The last time I saw him, he was leaving to go down to the cellar,' replied the psychiatrist.

'I know,' said Hallahan, his face pale. 'I tried to find him at one point, but with no success. It was just before I came back here. I hope—.'

The history professor didn't complete his sentence. He went into the corridor and called out to his friend several times. The only answer came from the wind. Bill and Jerrold joined him and added their voices, but with no better result. A dreadful apprehension seized them. Hallahan picked up the poker from the hearth and announced firmly:

'Let's take a look at the cellar.'

The sinister groan from the door which led there seemed like an ominous sign to Madge, and she was not mistaken: after having taken a few steps, Hallahan stumbled, faltered for a moment, then crashed down the stone steps. He cried out at the same time the lamp extinguished itself, plunging them into total darkness. There was a moment of utter confusion, but the voice of Bill could be heard above the tumult, asking them to stay still and wait for his return.

It wasn't long before Madge spotted, with immense relief, the moving light of a lamp.

At the base of the steps, the professor was moaning as he held his heel. While Madge held the lamp, Dr. Jerrold and Bill helped him up. He took a few steps, then shook his head sadly:

'I think I've broken something.'

After a swift examination, the doctor was reassuring:

'I don't think it's serious. A bad sprain, at the worst.'

'But I can't walk.'

'Just wait for a second. We'll take you back to the lounge.'

Once installed on the throne, Hallahan, his face drawn, urged the others to continue their search. The disappearance of his friend was more worrying than the state of his ankle. It was decided that Madge, armed with the poker, would stay with him while Bill and Jerrold would return to the hunt.

Five minutes after their departure, Madge pricked up her ears.

'Didn't you hear anything?' she asked her companion.

Hallahan frowned.

'Now you mention it. What is it?'

'It sounds like something sliding.'

Madge went pale as she indicated the door to the corridor, which had been left open:

'I think it's coming from over there.'

'Yes, and it's getting closer. Give me your poker, miss.'

'No, I'll keep it. You won't be able to use it.'

The young woman had pronounced the words firmly, but the expression on her face betrayed the mounting terror she felt as the sliding approached, accompanied by the revealing noise of heavy breathing.

She held her improvised weapon in both hands as something moved in the doorway to the corridor. A long, thin, shiny object which they recognised immediately: *the long blade of a sword, with the tip spattered with blood.*

20

Blake wasn't in the cellar. Bill and Jerrold became rapidly convinced of that. The psychiatrist observed that, if he had been in that part of the building, he would definitely have heard their calls.

'Unless he ran into the madman,' suggested Bill lugubriously.

'Let's wait before we assume the worst.'

'On the contrary, we have to. We're in a situation where we can't afford the slightest error. Besides, didn't Blake challenge Horatio several times by announcing his desire for a fight? If our man overheard him, he would certainly make it a point of honour to eliminate him first.'

Jerrold nodded his head slowly.

'Yes,' he sighed, 'that would certainly be in character. But how could he have overheard us? We battened down the whole castle. He wasn't there… at least, until he broke the window.'

'About that broken window,' said Bill pensively.

'Yes?'

'Did you examine it?'

'Not really.'

'I may be wrong, but…. Well, let's talk about that later. First we need to find Blake.'

'Suppose he went over to the tower?'

Ten minutes later, the two men were rapidly climbing the spiral staircase, vainly calling out to their friend who, they were about to discover, wasn't in the tower room either.

'So, now what do we do?' said Bill in angry frustration. 'He didn't leave the castle and he hasn't answered our calls.'

'You're right, we should fear the worst,' said the psychiatrist, mechanically checking the contents of the chest under the window. 'But I can't believe that a beefy fellow like Blake didn't put up a fight. Under normal circumstances we should have heard the noise from such a confrontation. We're in the presence of a diabolical murderer. He's so sure of himself he's playing cat and mouse with us.

Sometimes I have the impression he's spying on us, as if there were a thousand invisible eyes following our movements and savouring our anguish.'

Bill nodded his head.

'I get the same impression. And I also think, although it seems impossible, that we've locked him inside the castle with us.'

'Where is he, then?'

'You know, Doctor, these old walls hide many secrets. Maybe a secret passage or a hidey-hole which allows him to appear and disappear at will. But, instead of trying to track the monster down, there may be a better way to flush him out.'

Dr. Jerrold frowned.

'I think,' continued Bill, 'that such a person must be very conceited, wouldn't you say?'

'Obviously. Boundless conceit, coupled with an obsession with the epic, are the very roots of his madness. What's your idea?'

'Let's get back to the others and we'll talk about it.'

The patch of light they could see once they regained the ground floor corridor indicated that the door to the lounge was still open.

They entered the room and stopped dead. Gail Blake's massive body lay on the tiled floor under the shocked stares of Madge and Hallahan. His face was frozen in an expression of extreme agony and his hands were clutching the "sword in the stone" whose tip was spattered with blood. There was a large dark patch on his shirt around the abdomen.

21

'I think he only just died,' murmured Madge in a lifeless voice.

'What happened?' gulped Bill, rushing over to her as she burst into tears. 'Where's the madman? Have you seen him?'

'No,' replied an ashen Hallahan. 'But we did think it was he who was coming to get us, when we saw the blade of the sword appear in the doorway. We were wrong, it was Blake. He was grimacing horribly and had great difficulty walking. He took a few steps toward us, then crashed to the floor right there.'

'He's dead,' announced Jerrold, kneeling by the body. 'Killed most probably with the sword he's holding.'

'Killed?' repeated Hallahan, puzzled. 'But if he's holding it in his hand....'

'He must have pulled it out of the wound himself. He had the strength—and the courage—necessary. Unless the murderer, after plunging the weapon into his stomach, pulled it out and left it next to the victim. Blake could have picked it up before dragging himself here. Did you hear any noises of a fight?'

Madge and Hallahan shook their heads.

It didn't take Bill and Dr. Jerrold long to find the scene of the crime. Drops of blood led them along the corridor and—after they lit their lamps—to the door leading to the tower.

'The killer must have been behind the door,' declared Jerrold. 'He must have struck when Blake went in. It's pitch black in here. With the effect of surprise and the sword thrust swiftly into the belly, he wouldn't have been able to defend himself. What's certain is, with that wound, he wouldn't have been able to cry out. The pain must have been atrocious, and it's astonishing that he was able to pull the sword out and make it all the way to the lounge. But, as we know, the man had unusual strength and willpower.'

'Which didn't help him much with this monster,' observed Bill. 'We have to put this wild beast out of action before he eliminates us one by one.'

'Six.'

'Sorry?'

'Six. There are only six of us left. We have to warn the others, that's to say Dunbar, because Miss Brown, after what I gave her, will be sleeping like a log now.'

Five minutes later, having visited Ursula's room, Dr. Jerrold returned to the lounge.

'Dunbar has decided not to leave her side before the arrival of the forces of order,' he declared with a sigh. 'The news of the latest murder has almost driven him insane. If there weren't so few of us, I would have given him a sleeping pill. He's barricaded himself in her room. He double-locked the door when I left, and I heard him pushing the wardrobe against the door, as he said he would. In any case, somebody has to watch over Miss Brown. I think it's time to take stock and, above all, decide on a strategy. But it seems as though Mr. Page might already have one?'

'Bill,' exclaimed Madge suddenly, 'I want you to explain the mystery of the magic sword and the famous Grail to us before anything else.'

'Don't you think there are more urgent things to talk about?' asked her fiancé, standing next to the body of Gail Blake.

'Perhaps, but I don't want to die before I know.'

Bill was startled:

'Die before you know? My God, you're not very optimistic... or you have a strange sense of humour.'

'I must know.'

'How do you expect us to be optimistic, young man?' asked Josiah Hallahan, staring fixedly at the body of his friend. We're trapped inside an "invisible circle" and prisoners of a madman who's hell-bent on acting out the macabre play he's written. And he's here with us, witness that broken window over there.'

Dr. Jerrold turned to Bill:

'*A propos* the window, weren't you going to tell me something about it, just now?'

Bill nodded, went over to the window, and looked at the floor beneath it.

'At first blush, looking at the glass debris, it would appear that our killer came from outside because, obviously, if he'd smashed the window from inside, the vast majority of the glass debris would be outside and that is quite clearly not the case. Still, it would have been easy to pull the wool over our eyes while acting from inside. You first break one pane of glass, then grab hold of the lead frame and shake it violently, and the result is what you see here: glass debris on the floor and a twisted frame. Thus, *a priori*, there's no way of telling whether the act was committed from inside or out. Now look more closely at the lead lattice. It's been manhandled and it's twisted, but there's no sign of a physical blow. Notice also that the deformation is angled towards the inside. It's hard to imagine anyone from outside getting rid of this obstacle by pushing like that. Either he would have got rid of the entire window by smashing it with something hard, or he would have pulled it violently towards him. Neither of which we see here.'

'You—you're saying he's always been inside the castle?' stammered Madge.

'Even without imagining a secret passage,' replied Bill, 'someone extremely crafty who knew the place well could remain out of sight by playing hide-and-seek. Yes, I believe the killer never left the castle. And, by the way, even before the window was broken, there were shutters and doors slamming as if by magic. As I say, we can't be sure, but I believe he never left us for a minute.'

Judging from the rapt silence, everyone there agreed with Bill, who suddenly turned to stare at the sword still in the hands of the corpse. He asked Dr. Jerrold to prise it free and examine it. The psychiatrist, intrigued, complied.

'You want to know the mystery of the sword? Very well, there it is, in front of you. But tell us, Doctor, is it the same one? Do our inscriptions appear on the grip?'

'Yes, there's no doubt about it.'

'Very well. Now please bring me the Holy Grail.'

'The Holy Grail?' repeated the doctor, looking around in surprise. But, it disappeared, as you very well know.'

'You're mistaken. *You're holding it!*'

22

'The Grail... in my hands?' exclaimed Jerrold, staring at the sword in utter incomprehension.

'Yes, look at the grip, or rather the guard. It's golden, shiny and hemispherical, just like the cup which the false Gerry Pearson, alias Horatio, let us glimpse. Come over here. I'll hold the blade and you can try to unscrew the guard.'

'I already tried,' said Hallahan. 'It didn't budge.'

'I remember,' agreed Jerrold. 'It was in the tower room, when the false Inspector Roy asked us to examine it and check its solidity.'

'I'm sure you only tried to unscrew it in the conventional direction,' replied Bill, 'that's to say anti-clockwise. Try it the other way, as if you're trying to tighten it.'

It was only after several attempts that the guard started to move, after which it was easy to unscrew it from the blade. At the opposite end of the blade from the tip was a threaded shank about four inches long.

'Incredible,' said Bill, with an admiring whistle. 'He even went to the trouble of making a thread in the opposite sense to normal. And there's the key to the whole mystery: a guard and grip which can be screwed and unscrewed. And the killer, in the guise of Inspector Roy, even had the incredible audacity to point out the metal shavings next to the pillar drill which he had used to doctor the sword, and also the tapping tools. It was a superb piece of trickery for, as you've noticed, you can only unscrew the guard by exerting considerable pressure on it.'

While Jerrold, Hallahan and Madge stared at the guard, grip and pommel—the "Grail"—as if hypnotised, Bill continued his explanations, not without a tinge of pride.

'All we have to do to understand the hocus-pocus is to remember the sequence of events. It's when he feigns the pain in his wrist that he leaves this room with you, Madge, before disappearing for a short while and returning with the "Grail". He needs less than ten minutes to get to the "sword in the stone," unscrew the precious grip bearing the inscriptions later used to formally identify the sword, and use the large stake –which Miss Brown had almost tripped over—to topple the stone into the sea. The stone in which the blade of the sword remains embedded. He returns to show us the mysterious object which he pretends is the Grail. He lets us glimpse its golden radiance and round form, then places it on the chest—which, remember is under the window.

'The rest follows as I've already explained. He climbs up the rope and executes his accomplice, but with a different blade-without-a-grip, identical to the one lying on the reefs below the waves. He holds his victim's body with its back pressed against the grill, lights the material soaked in meths, pushes the body away from the wall slightly, picks up the "Grail" from the chest, screws it tightly onto the blade of the sword and pushes the body as far as possible into the room. All these manoeuvres are possible just by passing your hands through the iron grill, as I've personally verified. And *voila!* the trick is done. When we find the sword driven into the back of the victim, we're all prepared to swear it's the same one which was embedded in the stone.'

'You have to be completely and utterly insane to dream up such a stratagem,' murmured Hallahan, still staring at the "Grail."

'Insane, but extremely intelligent,' added Dr. Jerrold. 'In a way, the man's a sort of genius. His case is a very interesting one….'

'But also a very dangerous one,' replied Hallahan tersely. 'I don't feel any admiration whatsoever for him.'

'What, a great lover of Arthurian legends like yourself? That's surprising.'

'How can you still joke about this, Jerrold? To all intents and purposes, we're completely at his mercy.'

'I don't think he'd dare attack us while we're all together.'

Hallahan's smile was anything but friendly:

'You, of course, have the use of your legs. You can run, whereas I can hardly walk. If there's to be another victim, it'll be me. That's what you're thinking, isn't it?'

'How dare you make such a remark,' retorted Jerrold with an air of outraged dignity.

'But afterwards, it'll be your turn. And, besides, don't forget the fellow didn't hesitate to attack several people at once during that tragic incident in the theatre. You aren't any safer than I am, Doctor.'

'Did I say anything to the contrary?'

'You're a hypocrite, Dr. Jerrold!'

The psychiatrist, his face ashen, turned and walked out of the room.

A lengthy silence followed his departure. Hallahan made his way painfully over to the throne and sat down; he suddenly looked much older.

'My God, what's happening to me? It's ages since I insulted one of my peers. Dr. Jerrold is afraid, and I was beside myself when he made that fatuous remark. What I didn't realise immediately is that it was a way of giving himself courage. I flew off the handle, which was ridiculous. "Merlin the Enchanter" wasn't worthy of the name.'

'All our nerves are on edge,' said Madge, going over to him. 'I'm sure the doctor regrets leaving in a huff.'

"An irrational act," thought Hallahan, who was careful not to give voice to the thought. "Wandering around alone, with things the way they are, is pure folly. He'll be back soon."

Hallahan was right. Shortly thereafter, Dr. Jerrold reappeared, albeit hesitantly.

'The sensible thing to do,' he said, swallowing his pride, 'is for us all to remain calm.'

A few minutes later, the incident was forgotten and the psychiatrist reminded Bill that he'd talked about a plan to put the monster out of action.

'I was getting to that,' said Bill mysteriously. 'In fact, the idea would be to set a trap for him and lure him in. I know it's risky, but I fear that if we just stay here, just parrying his blows, we'll soon be reduced to counting the corpses. But before we go any further, Dr. Jerrold, I'd like you to sketch a psychological portrait of this man. You're clearly the one best placed to do it, and it's very important.'

'I'm beginning to see,' said the psychiatrist, with a knowing air. 'Let me say, for a start, that this kind of personality is one of the hardest to treat, and therefore to understand. Obviously, his obsessions are clear and he doesn't bother to hide them. His homicidal mania is also evident. He kills because he likes killing. In general, in these cases, we're dealing with subjects who are driven purely by their impulses and therefore are relatively easy to control. But Horatio is notable for a lively intelligence, which he puts to use during his off-peak periods—if you'll forgive the expression—which make him a particularly formidable adversary. He's clearly very conscious of his power and intelligence, which he wants to be known and admired. And that's the aspect which interests you, I suspect, Mr. Page?'

Bill nodded.

'I haven't studied his case personally,' Jerrold continued. 'Like everyone else, I've followed it through press reports. In addition to the obvious arrogance and vanity, there's also a form of narcissism, of self-admiration, so to speak, for his "work." Everything in the last forty-eight hours proves it. It's a spectacular, tremendous show he's put on for us. Great art! The most surprising and agonising effects. And everything founded on the marvellous, on the Arthurian legend.'

'And he's very proud of it,' observed Bill.

'There's no doubt of that.'

'It's a subject he wouldn't want us to joke about....'

'Absolutely not! It's eminently serious and worthy of interest.'

Bill nodded his head several times before speaking in a low voice:

'Here's what I propose. We're going to go along with his game and *play Knights of the Round Table with him*. Perform a short piece the way he likes them, in such a way he won't be able to resist joining in. We'll lure him to the tower and shut him in. Two of us perform a loud scene up in the tower room while the others lie in wait below.

'As soon as he sets foot in the tower, they'll seal the door from the outside by passing a heavy chain through the ring which serves as a door knocker. The tower is a veritable prison: we've sealed every opening.'

'But the others,' said Madge nervously, 'the ones already in the room, won't they be shut in with him?'

'Yes, but not at his mercy, because they'll be solidly barricaded in. I know the door is damaged at the moment, but a few solid planks nailed across it will transform that room into an impregnable fortress. And our prey will be caught in a trap.'

'It's a good plan, but very risky,' observed Hallahan thoughtfully. 'What do you think, Jerrold?'

'As far as luring him into the trap, I think it can't fail, provided the "scene" is well acted. As for the rest, I fear that the slightest error could be fatal. How do you see the division of the roles?'

Bill looked at the ceiling:

'Dunbar doesn't seem operational, not to mention Miss Brown. In my view, we can only really count on the four of us.'

'Agreed,' said Jerrold impatiently, 'but who's going to be the bait, up there?'

Bill turned slowly towards Madge:

'You and I, darling. That is, if you agree.'

The young woman opened her mouth, but no sound came out.

'I think it's the best formula, Madge, and there's virtually no risk because we'll be barricaded in. Let me explain your role and you'll see it's the best way to attract Horatio. Don't forget his game, where you theoretically play the part of Guinevere, Arthur's wife. He, Horatio, is the vengeful King Arthur, of course. He assigned me the role of Lancelot, your lover. We'll play a love scene, naturally, but one where we quarrel. Lancelot accuses his mistress of something, voices are raised and he insults her and starts to maltreat her. We'll talk very loudly and you, Madge, will scream. I'm sure that, at that point, "Arthur" wont be able to resist intervening to defend his wife—whom he still loves—and punishing the treacherous knight.'

'Excellent,' commented Jerrold. 'Excellent from a psychological point of view. He'll intervene, it's almost certain.'

'And once he sets foot in the tower, that'll be where you come in, gentlemen. You have to act fast to shut him in by sealing the main door.'

'I'll do what I can with my poor ankle,' said Hallahan. 'It's really up to you, doc.'

'It has to be done quickly and precisely. I'm not going to let you down.'

'I'll follow you, Bill,' said Madge bravely, with tears in her voice.

'Right!' thundered Bill. 'Let's not waste any more time. The die is cast!'

23

It was two o'clock when Madge and Bill crossed the tower threshold. The old wooden door emitted its customary lugubrious groan. Bill was carrying planks and a large bag of tools, and Madge a bag of provisions. The climb up was even slower than usual, for Horatio could well have been lurking nearby.

Once in the room, they put down their bags and Madge threw herself into Bill's arms.

'My God, I can't wait for this nightmare to end,' she moaned. 'I'm completely at the end of my tether.'

'Don't worry, darling, it'll be over soon, trust me. But first we have to repair the door.'

'Repair it? But I thought we were going to nail planks across it?'

'We're going to strengthen it and screw on this large bolt I brought. We have to be able to leave when we need to. I'll explain later. But let's get to work.'

Madge stared wide-eyed at her fiancé.

'I get the impression you're hiding something from me.'

'I'll explain everything. But first the door.'

A quarter of an hour later, a massive new bolt had been screwed in place.

'And now, darling, we're going to start our play, and while we're acting, I'll explain things in a low voice. I'll tell you straight away I'm afraid we've been completely fooled by the killer.'

'I don't understand,' murmured Madge, who had not taken her eyes off her fiancé.

'Let's start. We'll go over by the window so he can hear us better. Ready? I'll use my stentorian voice:

'Guinevere, my sweet, there you are at last. I've been waiting for you for an hour in the garden and I was beginning to think you'd forgotten our rendezvous.'

Madge cleared her throat before replying:

'How can you think such a thing, my sweet friend? I was detained at table.'

'Detained by whom?'

'By Arthur.'

'That's what I feared.'

'If you please?'

'You attach little importance to your humble servant.'

'Lancelot, your words are like darts planted in my heart. I was detained by Arthur because it was his wish.' Then, lowering her voice: 'Now, Bill, explain to me….'

'Because it was his wish? Would he have kept you by force? Cavalier manners indeed for one of such high rank. It's simple: I've good reason to believe the criminal who's been terrifying us isn't Horatio.'

'What? Horatio isn't… I don't understand anything anymore. So, then, who is it?'

'Don't forget your role, Madge. I'm still trying to work out who the guilty party is. Or, rather, I think I know who it is, but I don't know which mask he's hiding behind.'

'Stop speaking in riddles, Bill, for heaven's sake.'

'Play your part, Madge.'

'Umm… Where were we?'

'I said Arthur had detained you by force.'

'Yes… But… But Arthur did not detain me by force. He suspects something… I should not be surprised if the hand of Mordred were behind all this. I have surprised him several times whispering in Arthur's ear. He stops when he sees my regard.'

'It is easy to blame Mordred. Methinks it is you, my fair lady, who tires of me. Do you remember just now, when I showed how the glass was broken from the inside? I talked about Horatio playing hide-and-seek, but I was actually gauging their reactions. The killer is someone in our little group, I'm sure of it. The fact I stressed the way the glass had been broken must have attracted the attention of the one who did it: the killer.'

'Who is it? Be careful, my friend, if you insist so much, I may end by believing it.'

'I insist. You are tired of me.'

'Who is it, Bill? *So be it, then: I shall be frank with you: I do not love you any more, Lancelot.*'

'I'll tell you afterwards. You'll understand better then.' In a voice dripping with scorn: *'Thus was I not mistaken. I take pity on you, Guinevere.'*

'You do love to have your little secrets, don't you? Very well. Here goes: *And I, I hate you, I hate you, I hate you.* So, if I understand correctly, the person you're trying to trap isn't Horatio at all!'

'Horatio is dead. He's the one who was murdered in this room, and he's the one who welcomed us and played the part of your uncle.'

'So, he was an accomplice.'

'Yes, but a special kind of accomplice, one easily manoeuvred if you went about it the right way. An important trump card in the murderer's plan. *At last, my dear, your true nature has been exposed.*'

'My true nature? And what would that be?'

'You are deceit itself. And, did I not restrain myself—.'

'How dare you, base and vile person! Bill, if you don't tell me right now who the killer is, I shall scream.'

'Go ahead, darling. Feel free. *Here, take this slap. And another one for good measure.*'

'You're a horrible person.' She emitted a piercing scream.

'Excellent. You'd make a fine actress, darling. I'll give you a clue: the murderer is Peter Cobb!'

'The young watchman? But....'

'The truth is, the murderer acted the part, like so many others during these last hours. Do you remember his testimony? It was a bit over the top, didn't you think? The ghost of King Arthur who murders a fake police officer before vanishing as if by magic. The whole thing was a fairy tale.'

'There were so many extraordinary things. What was one more?'

'You're not saying anything, my dear. But you're trembling. You're afraid, aren't you. Do you believe that coward Arthur will come to your aid? He is too afraid of me. And now, Madge, I need you to perform a short monologue, to give me time to go downstairs and check something out.'

'What? You want to leave me alone here? *What do you say? That Arthur is a coward? There is no worse insult.*'

'I won't be long, I promise.'

'But what for?'

'You want to get the nightmare over with, don't you? Then let me do it. I need to execute a certain manoeuvre down below. *Yes, I say it loud and clear. Arthur is nothing but a coward and always has been.*'

'Bill, I beg you, don't take any risks.'

'Trust me. Wait, let me give you something.'

He picked a large kitchen knife out of his tool bag and gave it to the young woman.

'That's all I could find to defend ourselves with. You won't need to use it, but you'll feel safer.'

Madge took the knife and looked fearfully at the large shiny blade.

'Bill,' she implored, 'at least tell me who?'

'Come now, haven't you worked it out? The demonic personage who played successively the parts of Peter Cobb, Inspector Roy, and now a third one? The creature who killed Horatio the Mad, the poor devil whom we knew as Sergeant Hunt… and now Blake. I'm sure you know it in your heart, that you've intuitively felt it, Madge. Well, I'm off. Be sure to lock the door behind me, you never know. I'll be gone for five minutes at most. I'm sure you'll be able to improvise for that long.'

'Who is it, Bill? You still haven't told me.'

'Gerry Pearson, your beloved uncle.'

24

The rain-laden wind which swept the dark courtyard carried snatches of Madge's speech:

'I hate you... Lancelot... I hate you....'

Motionless in one corner, Hallahan lay in wait. His eyes still hadn't got accustomed to the pitch darkness. He sensed rather than saw the tower door, some twenty steps away. At his feet lay the chain and padlock to be used for holding the murderer in the tower.

'How dare you, Lancelot... to him... to him, the bravest of knights,' continued Madge's voice from afar.

An approaching footstep caused him to jump and he saw a shadow approaching, which turned out to be none other than Dr. Jerrold.

'You've been long enough,' murmured the professor reproachfully.

'I wanted to check something, but I think I wasted my time.'

'Don't speak so loudly.'

'Guess who I saw in the corridor, going down to the cellar.'

'Horatio?'

'No, don't worry. It was none other than Dunbar.'

'What was he doing?'

'I didn't tackle him. He seemed in a hurry. I don't think he saw me.'

'Bizarre. And he left Miss Brown on her own?'

'Obviously.'

Jerrold straightened up suddenly:

'What was that scream? Did you hear it?'

'It's our young couple acting out their play. Guinevere has just been slapped by Lancelot.'

'Have they started already? One can hardly hear a thing.'

'It depends which way the wind is blowing.'

'Do you think *he* will hear them?'

'We'll see. You were saying Miss Brown was alone in her room.'

'That's what held me up. I thought I'd better check. I went up and knocked discreetly at her door, but with no result. It was locked.'

'So she was inside.'

'Doubtless, but I didn't dare knock any louder.'

'She must be sleeping like a log. What you gave her was quite powerful, wasn't it?'

'To calm her down and help send her to sleep, yes, but it wasn't an anaesthetic. If something wakes her up, she'll quickly recover... Sh! I just heard a noise.'

For several seconds, all that could be heard was the wailing of the wind. Hallahan and Dr. Jerrold, remaining perfectly still and holding their breath, tried to penetrate the darkness of the courtyard. They could hear a faraway hubbub coming from the tower, followed by the sound of footsteps. Then, a few seconds later, they noticed a shadow moving close to the wall near the tower door and heard the familiar groaning noise shortly thereafter.

Several seconds passed before Hallahan murmured in his companion's ear:

'Did you see it?'

'Only just.'

'What do we do?'

'Wait, I hear more footsteps.'

'You're right. But, Hell's bells, what's happening? Who are all these people?'

'Sh... he's coming. Look... there... he just left by the door of the main building. He... no, it's a woman!'

'Miss Brown, I believe. What the devil's she doing here? She's turning back. Stay here, Hallahan, I'm going to get a closer look.'

'Leave here, Lancelot, I order you,' shouted Madge, standing near the open window. *Out of my sight.'*

She stopped suddenly, alerted by a sound.

A step on the stairs.

Firmly grasping the kitchen knife in both hands, she retreated as far from the door as possible, her eyes riveted on the new bolt.

It was only when she heard four knocks on the door—the signal pre-arranged with Bill—and heard the voice of her companion that she felt sufficiently reassured to open the door.

Bill came in and she immediately moved to bolt the door behind him. It was stiff and she had to strain to move it. She turned in response to Bill's call and failed to notice that the bolt had failed to engage properly, even though the door appeared to be shut.

'Darling, hand me the knife. You're going to injure yourself like that.'

'Now, Bill, you're going to explain everything. Do you understand? Everything.'

Bill took the knife, looked at it for a moment, then went over to the window and shouted:

'No, Guinevere, you can't get out of it like that. Do you think I'm going to leave the matter there? Certainly not. As for your husband, the royal poltroon, I'll meet him squarely. That is, if he dares show his face.'

'Don't you think we can stop this tomfoolery, Bill? After all, it serves no purpose if Horatio is dead.'

'Obviously, but the others need to think we're still playing the game. *But you're mad, Madam. You dared to strike me, Lancelot. You shall pay dearly for this.'*

'You'll surely not hit a defenceless woman.'

'And why not, if she deserves it.'

Madge emitted a scream fit to wake the dead, then Bill said:

'Let's not overdo it. I suggest a short pause.'

'Now tell me who is Uncle Gerry. I have to know.'

'You'll know in a few moments, darling, I promise you.'

Madge stiffened:

'You mean he's coming here?'

'Yes, in a manner of speaking. Now, please try not to interrupt me all the time.'

Madge, on the verge of tears, went over to snuggle in Bill's arms. He said soothingly:

'The nightmare will soon be over for you, Madge. Didn't it ever occur to you that the person behind all the diabolical machinations was your uncle? Surely you must have suspected it.'

'You're probably right.'

'He's the only one capable of such a tortuous scheme. He's a perverse individual, and you and Miss Brown rightly judged him so.'

'He's abominable. Yes, I felt it. I felt his presence when we were in the library. He was next to me, playing the part of Inspector Roy. My instinct told me there was danger.'

'First of all, you need to know he's not insane and he's following a pre-determined plan. That crazy and macabre stage production, with all its twists and turns up to the discovery of the fake policeman, had only one goal: to make you believe—which you all did—that Horatio the Mad was behind it all. That he was recreating the carnage he had wrought a few years earlier. The fact that he'd just been released from the asylum, that he was a gifted actor and a lover of the Arthurian legends, led everyone to believe he must be the monster behind the hellish weekend.

'He was Gerry Pearson's accomplice, as I told you. He was the one who welcomed us and who played the role of our strange and disturbing host, but he was obeying the orders of your uncle, who had no trouble convincing him to participate in the farce—which he undoubtedly enjoyed. It was made to measure: playing a caricature of his own personality! He was clearly unaware Gerry was planning to kill him. Everything went according to plan. The crime was acrobatic and dangerous, yes, but your uncle had had all the time in the world to practice and perfect it *chez lui*. There was a reason to disfigure his half-brother's face, because he was supposed to be the guilty party at first; but the real guilty party had only just begun to play with his guinea-pigs. We were supposed to think the victim was someone Horatio had known in the asylum.'

'But why, for heaven's sake, did he do all that? Why?'

'Why?' repeated Bill with a curious smile. 'Because it was in his interests. But we're forgetting about our scene.' He went over to the window and shouted:

'Ah! You've come to your senses. What? You wish me to stop striking you? For what reason, pray tell.'

Madge provided the obligatory heart-breaking screams and continued:

'In his interests? I don't understand.'

'Your uncle needs money. Lots of it. The castle costs a lot to run, particularly if he wants to restore it to his taste.'

While Madge continued to look perplexed, Bill fished an envelope out of his jacket pocket.

'My letter!' she exclaimed. 'Where did you find it?'

'You should have read it. It's from a solicitor requesting your presence to verify your identity. Your father, who did not die as thought, finally made his fortune. He passed away recently from a tropical disease and left you quite a pretty penny.'

Madge, thunderstruck, stammered:

'Left—Left it to me?'

'Which you inherit,' continued her fiancé, 'provided you don't die beforehand.'

'Bill....'

'You're starting to understand Uncle Gerry's plan.'

'Bill, he must be on the stairs. I can hear footsteps.'

'No, he's not on the stairs.'

'Yes, Bill. He's not far away, I can feel it.'

'The whole macabre comedy was staged to hide the true motive, which was to eliminate you, while placing the responsibility for the massacre on his half-brother. Then he needed to be eliminated so Uncle Gerry would become the sole heir. He now only needs to commit the final act, which is to kill you—to stab you the way Horatio the Mad would have done.'

'It's monstrous. Bill, I think he's very close.'

Arming himself with the knife, Bill stood by the door. He placed his ear against it, then straightened up. He walked slowly towards Madge, with an unrecognisable smile on his face.

'You're right, Madge. Uncle Gerry's not far away. He's close to you. In this room, in fact....'

Instinctively, Madge looked round the room. Then the awful truth dawned on her.

Bill had stopped in front of her, brandishing the large kitchen knife. He let out a terrifying laugh:

'And stop screaming, Guinevere. It's no use. But you can start, darling. Yes, that's right... I'm Uncle Gerry.'

25

Madge felt her legs go weak and her head spin. She was living a nightmare, a dreadful nightmare.

'Now you understand what I meant when I said the nightmare would soon be over for you,' sneered Bill, alias Gerry Pearson.

"How can humanity have produced someone so ugly," thought Madge, whose revulsion at the loathsome being in front of her had overcome her fear. Could this monster have found a more credulous being than her? She doubted it. Now she understood why he had appeared to be prematurely aging: in fact, he wasn't thirty, but in his mid-forties.

And he'd been able to read her like an open book.

'They say the sea air ages you, but I must be the exception which proves the rule, for I haven't got many wrinkles. Why didn't you recognise me? First of all, it's due to my talent: I was able to change my personality without using make-up. As for you, your memories of me were of a nasty man twice the size of the little girl you were at the time. I'm pretty good at playing the discreet and serious young leading man, don't you think?'

Madge had to force herself not to try and attack the odious creature.

'As I say, feel free to scream. Do you understand the purpose of the argument between Lancelot and Guinevere now? Subtle, isn't it? Your uncle has always been someone very subtle.'

'You're not my uncle. There's no blood relationship at all between us. I was adopted by my parents and, by the way, you're only the half-brother of my adoptive father.'

Pearson contented himself with a smile:

'Let's talk about your father, because I want you to know everything. You will have the signal privilege of knowing all the details of my plan, a veritable jewel of its kind. A unique privilege, alas! because I can't share it with anyone else.

'Your father, as you know, left to make his fortune in Africa. But, having rapidly disappeared, his friends there all assumed he was dead.

A few months ago, I received a letter from him—shortly before his untimely death from one of those unforgiving tropical illnesses, in fact. He had led a very eventful life, wounded by natives, saved by others, betrayed by a "faithful" friend after he found the deposits he had searched for so long, and so on. But he did at last find his gold mine: a river bed full of nuggets as big as those which made the ancient king of Lydia's fortune. He didn't become Croesus, but almost. He left behind enough to live comfortably on until the end of his days. You might ask why he gave no sign of life all that time. In the beginning, he was unable to. Afterwards, when he learned he'd been written off as dead, he swore he would only return with his pockets full of gold. Too bad he was felled by that illness at the last moment.

'Too bad for you, that is. Because your dear old Uncle Gerry decided to take a hand. What would you have done with all that money anyway? You'd have let yourself be bamboozled by the first Don Juan who came along, who would have fleeced you in less time than it takes to tell. No, I thought long and hard about it: the money would be better used by Uncle Gerry, who would at last be able to restore his castle as he saw fit.'

'Completely cuckoo,' muttered Madge, through clenched teeth.

'Mad or bad,' mocked the lord of the manor. 'Which is it? It's Horatio who was mad! It was when I learnt of your father's death that I formulated my plan. A complex, carefully worked-out plan which demanded a long preparation. But it was worth it, I'm sure you'll agree. You do understand, I trust? For, with you out of the way, I'm the sole remaining heir. However, should you die a violent death, with that fortune at risk, I would be the prime suspect. So, an elaborate plan had to be put in place to deflect suspicion. Horatio's propitious release created the ideal smokescreen, given his history of homicidal madness. Who, shocked by the horror of this new carnage, even more insane than the previous incident, would suspect any other motive? Act one: seduce you....'

'You make me sick,' murmured Madge, as the revolting personage continued.

'... which wasn't all that difficult, I must say. Next, filling the place up over the weekend. I invited several colourful people, and also that cow Ursula and her old boyfriend, so as to spice things up. A specialist in mental illness seemed like a good idea. By the way, the story of the young woman incarcerated by way of revenge is totally untrue. Dr. Jerrold has the reputation of an intransigent specialist, that's all.

'If anyone had turned my invitation down, I had replacements in reserve. But everyone came. By the way, the cold buffet was prepared by a cook in the village who knows me well. I took the precaution of sending Horatio to deal with her. That way, when questioned later, she could say how bizarre she'd found me that day.

'Previously, I'd collected Horatio secretly from the asylum and brought him home, in order to prepare him for the role I wanted him to play. I must admit he's a very gifted actor, almost as gifted as I myself, as you have come to realise. Remember Peter Cobb? An easy caricature: a dim-witted young man with gruff manners. Needless to say, the loss of my wallet was no accident. I reached the watchman's hut by taking that steep path around the rock, put on an old overcoat and a wig and *voila!* there was Peter Cobb waiting to greet you. Do you remember the conversation we had?'

'Only too well.'

'The "unpleasant business," to explain why the earlier arrivals hadn't seen me... Everything was planned down to the smallest detail. After that, Bill was delayed because of the luggage. That, I have to admit, was improvised. At no time did you see Peter and me together, and it's the same for "Inspector Roy." Not bad, eh? "Bill" left because "Inspector Roy" quickly despatched him to the village. If you had thought about it just now, when I said that "Uncle Gerry" was one of us, you should have rapidly concluded that it could only be me. I was the only one absent during "Inspector Roy's" performance.

'And what a performance it was, don't you agree? I led the investigation of my own crime, pointing out all the clues! We were in the workshop in the cellar when I noticed you tiptoe away. So, making an excuse about joining my colleague in the tower, I took the postern gate in order to get ahead of you and play the role of Peter again.'

'I did hear footsteps at the time.'

'You know what happened next: a terrified Peter describing an utterly fantastic murder, in order to give credence to the tale of the vengeful ghost. In fact, it was afterwards, when you went back to warn your colleagues, that I killed "Sergeant Hunt" up on the rocky promontory where we'd arranged to meet. "Sergeant Hunt" was another loony Horatio had met in the asylum. A completely harmless vegetable who lived on another planet. He did what he was asked without question. He'd even helped me to get rid of Horatio's body a bit earlier. We threw it into the sea—as was said---from the plateau where the famous sword had been planted. What with the tempest that night, and the reefs, there can't be much left of poor Horatio. An unrecognisable corpse, particularly since he was already disfigured by then.'

'That's enough! I don't want to hear any more.'

Gerry Pearson, alias Bill, pretended to be offended:

'What? Such a finely chiselled plan, so lovingly prepared? Try to make an effort. It's the home stretch, I promise.

'Taking the short-cut to the bridge again, I reached the village before you and that nitwit Blake, where I appeared as Bill. I won't go over all that again. What's left? Ah, yes, the shutters that slammed in the night. Ridiculously easy. All I had to do was fail to lock one when we were battening down the castle, and wait for the predictable gust of wind. Then—and you were with me at the time, while we were looking for the offending shutter—unlock others as I went round and leave the door leading to the courtyard ajar. As for the broken window, I did what I had described, which only took a few seconds: it had all been prepared. And, obviously, I killed that fat pig Blake without difficulty during the panic. I beckoned to him as he crossed the courtyard and ran him through with the sword. It's a pity, but it was too dark to see the expression of surprise in his eyes. He didn't cry out, just gave a deep groan. I didn't want to be too brutal. He pulled the sword out of his fat belly himself.

'And now, my dear Madge, we come to the end of the tale. Once this extraordinary weekend is over, the survivors—which obviously won't include you—will recount their misadventures to the police, describing how they managed to escape from Horatio the Mad, who accidentally fell over a cliff while being pursued. That's the final scene, which will happen shortly. The homicidal maniac who dies after imposing a reign of terror on his brother's island, that's what everyone will conclude. Your death, my dear niece, will be a mere detail amongst all the slaughter.'

'And where was Uncle Gerry all this time?'

'Staying up in London, with one of those alibis which are my trademark. You can rest assured, it will be cast-iron. Now I'm going to explain what happens next. Come closer....'

Madge recoiled suddenly, letting out a scream loud enough to shake the old stones of the tower.

'Here, take this, Guinevere! You can't escape, my beauty, it's impossible. Listen. Just now, I went downstairs to open and shut the door so that those nitwits there think that Horatio has arrived, so they can seal it. After getting rid of you, I shall simulate a fight and pound on the door for someone to open, on the pretext that the madman is after me. I'll run out and get the others to follow, and later there'll be a famous pursuit which will end with the so-called death of the so-called Horatio. And now....'

With unspeakable horror, Madge saw once more the terrible smile on the cruel face of the murderer. Gerry Pearson advanced slowly towards her; in his eyes was the same metallic reflection as on the large kitchen knife he was brandishing in front of him.

A long scream of terror pierced the night. It reached everywhere in the castle and on the island, and, for a few seconds, even drowned out the persistent moaning of the wind.

EPILOGUE

Gerry Pearson was not hanged, nor even judged, for his crimes. He died in the manner he had so carefully prepared for others: accidentally, falling from a cliff while being hounded by his pursuers.

'He escaped justice, but not his destiny,' declared Ursula, several years later in front of a few friends invited round for tea.

'My God, what a horrible story!' exclaimed a plump matron, putting her cup down in disgust, as if that respectable beverage was somehow implicated. 'What a horrible murderer! It's scarcely imaginable.'

'Yes, he was a frightful person,' replied Frank Dunbar, now a peaceful sixty-year old who had adapted to life since marrying the woman of his dreams. 'But at least he served one useful purpose, darling, during his time on this good old earth.'

'Really? That's quite a surprise,' replied Ursula, giving her husband a puzzled look.

'First of all, it's thanks to him that we're together. In fact, we should thank him twice. Without him, I would never have met you in the station that day, and without his invitation to that famous weekend, we would never have been reconciled. Which confirms my theory that every creature on this planet was put here for a purpose.'

Ursula smiled:

'I'd love to know what purpose I serve, according to you.'

'That's a delicate question if I ever heard one,' replied her husband roguishly. 'Isn't there an international convention which forbids spouses complimenting each other in public? But let me think... Yes, you did play an important role.'

'Do tell,' said the plump matron, who loved confidences almost as much as the *petit fours* on the plate in front of her.

'It's thanks to Ursula that the list of victims wasn't longer. The Pearson girl—who isn't a girl anymore—owes her her life.'

'Madge Pearson!' exclaimed Ursula. 'I can see her now, with her wide-eyed innocence. I wonder what's become of her?'

'Don't you know? She married a rich archaeologist.'

'So, that's her second husband.'

'Maybe. In any case, she's somewhere in the Middle East, in search of who knows which buried city. She's passionate about archaeology herself.'

'She's lucky to have married a rich man.'

It was Dunbar's turn to smile:

'She wasn't exactly poor herself, after inheriting her adoptive father's estate. But let's get back to you, Ursula, and the good deed which justifies your presence on the planet.'

'It was a question of intuition. You know, that little something which you men lack.'

'I'm not going to reopen that debate, darling,' said Frank, his mind going back to that terrible night....

He had just opened another bottle of whisky after the visit of Dr. Jerrold, who had come to inform him of Blake's murder. Seated patiently, he looked at Ursula who, in spite of the psychiatrist's sedatives, was still tossing and turning in her sleep. She had woken up once and he had broken the news of another murder. She had lapsed back into troubled sleep full of nightmares, when suddenly she had sat bolt upright with revulsion in her eyes.

'Frank,' she had said, staring blankly ahead, 'Gerry Pearson isn't dead.'

'Calm down, darling, you know it's his brother Horatio who—.'

'Gerry isn't dead, he's still alive, I recognised him. He's one of us. The one who calls himself Bill Page is really him.'

'Him, Gerry? But that's absurd. He's Madge's fiancé. How could his niece not have recognised him, but you with your poor vision—.'

'It's not about vision. I've just had a dream, where he appeared in his true light. But, in any case, I sensed it subconsciously. Gerry was around us all the time, somewhere. And now I'm sure: he's Bill.'

Faced with Ursula's insistence, Dunbar let himself be convinced. First, he went down to the cellar, to find something which could be used as a weapon. Then, together with Ursula, he went looking for the others. Alerted by the screams, they went into the little courtyard, where they found Dr. Jerrold and Hallahan, who explained the trap laid by Bill. After Ursula had told them of her suspicions and a terrifying scream had emanated from the tower, the truth hit them with an irresistible logic. With the exception of Hallahan, who could only manoeuvre with difficulty, they hurled themselves at the stairs leading to the tower room which, thanks to Madge's clumsiness, was not locked. They arrived just at the moment when Pearson, holding the young woman by her hair to better expose her throat, was about to strike the fatal blow. Ursula, driven by an unspeakable hatred, threw herself on the murderer. She would have received a fatal blow had not Dunbar delivered a devastating kick in the groin. Then, overcoming his natural reticence, Jerrold threw himself into the fray. The murderer, despite his energy, realised it would be impossible to overcome such unbridled fury.

He ran away. It was the start of a merciless manhunt which lasted two hours. His knowledge of the terrain was an advantage, but each time he pulled away from his pursuers, they were able to trace him by the drops of blood from the wounds caused by Ursula's ferocious attack. He was eventually caught in his own trap, unable to breach the "invisible circle." Driven to the top of the island, he slipped at the edge of a cliff. The reefs and the wild sea welcomed him a hundred feet below.

The next morning, alerted by a villager who had noticed the broken bridge, a number of policemen arrived on the island and the nightmare was over.

Dr. Jerrold kept a vivid recollection of his stay, the agony of which faded over time, but which elicited a lively interest when he recounted it to his friends. An account which evolved over the years and which increasingly emphasised his exceptional analytic faculties and his extraordinary understanding of human nature.

What happened to Josiah Hallahan, professor of history? After retiring, he returned to that old Celtic sod which he loved so much, there to live to the end of his days. And if you want to hear him recount one of the legends of the Round Table, ask Vivian: she will tell you where you can find him, within the magical invisible circle.

Made in the USA
Middletown, DE
04 January 2015